LOVE IN THE MOUNTAINS BOX SET

RAIN ON A TIN ROOF
LOST AND FOUND
RESCUE HIS HEART

Suzanne Cass

RAIN ON A TIN ROOF

Suzanne Cass

Dusty

'I found her,' Dusty said into his two-way radio. 'She's alive. Suffering from hypothermia. No other major injuries I can see. Over.' As he waited for a response from the SES handler he glanced up at the woman hunched over in the saddle on top of his horse. Hell, she was going to fall off Scout if she didn't stop swaying like a sapling in a breeze and he pushed his shoulder hard against her thigh. Scout shifted uneasily, apprehensive of the strange woman on his back. Dusty had already wrapped his oilskin coat around the woman's slim shoulders, but he needed to get her somewhere warm and dry. Soon. There was nasty weather on the way, he could see it in the low clouds and feel it in the biting wind.

She was awake when he found her, but glassy-eyed and barely talking, huddled next to an old fallen log like a desperate, wild animal. If Scout hadn't shied away from her dark shape, half-hidden by the long grass and low scrub, Dusty probably wouldn't have seen her. She'd been able to mumble something as he'd lifted her off the ground, but then her head lolled against his chest, semi-conscious.

'Easy,' Dusty growled and laid his palm flat against the appaloosa's neck. Scout snorted, but stood still, letting Dusty know he wasn't happy with this situation by showing the whites of his eyes.

3

'I know,' Dusty soothed the horse. 'Good boy.'

His two-way radio crackled to life. 'Message received. Did you say you found her? The missing woman, Ehlana Bingly? Over.'

'Yep, I've got her,' Dusty repeated. 'But I'm nearly out of daylight up here. And I think it's going to snow. I'm taking her to Kidman's Hut, on the eastern side of Mount Jagungal. Try and get her out of this freezing weather. Can you organize a team to meet us there? Over.'

'Message received. Is that you, Dusty? Dusty Hillman? Over.'

'Yes, John, it's Dusty here. Over.' John Reedman was well-known around town. A big man, friendly and determined, he helped out whenever he was needed. John did a good job of manning the Alpine State Emergency Services desk, keeping the volunteers up to date and on track in times of need, like now. He'd rallied the community together to organize this search for the missing woman.

'Didn't know you were part of this rescue, Dusty. She's one lucky lady. Thanks for joining us. Over.'

'Let me know how long it's going to take that team to get to us. Over,' he replied in clipped tones, cutting off any further conversation. It was too damn cold, and he was too damn pissed off to be swapping banter with John right now. Dusty led Scout over to a fallen log and hauled himself up behind the sagging woman. He gathered the reins in one hand and reached his other arm around her waist. Which wasn't hard to do. It was a tiny waist. Actually, she was a tiny woman, her head sat neatly beneath his chin as they rode.

'Don't you bloody well fall off, woman. I'm likely to leave you lying there in the grass if you do,' Dusty growled in a low voice. She made no sign of having heard him. Perhaps she would've replied if she knew how close to the truth that statement actually was.

What the hell was he doing here? Christ, he should be back on his farm bringing that last bunch of sheep down to the shelter of the home paddock before this bloody storm hit. He could lose the whole flock if he left them up in the high paddock. And what for? Just so he could rescue some bloody woman from the city. A woman who should've stayed in the city and who had no right being out here in the mountains in the first place.

Originally, he'd ignored the call for volunteers to join the search. The first call for help had gone out yesterday afternoon. He heard it when he went back to the house to make himself a coffee and get out of the biting cold for a few moments. The CB radio on top of his refrigerator was alive with chatter and calls from the SES, asking all able-bodied persons to come and help look for a woman who hadn't returned from a short horse ride into the foothills of the Snowy Mountains. Dusty stared out the grimy window pane into the brown paddocks and blew on his cup of coffee while he listened to the conversations of the community rallying behind the call. The mountains rose, dark and foreboding just behind the last line of trees on his property. Dusty was sure they'd find her before nightfall, she couldn't have gotten far. Besides, he had too much to do today. The fence over in Hanging Paddock needed to be fixed, before more of his sheep disappeared onto Sampson's property. So he stumped his Blundstone boots back onto his feet, shrugged on his well-worn oilskin coat and went back into the icy wind.

But next morning they still hadn't found her. As he listened over the radio the voices became more sombre and serious. The horse the woman had been riding reappeared at her uncle's farm, over on Bogong Flat. Not too far from Dusty's farm. The horse was completely exhausted, muddy and scratched, with saddle askew and reins broken and trailing on the ground. Which left the woman, Ehlana, on her own, out all night in freezing conditions. It seemed she wasn't even wearing a proper coat. Not a good scenario.

His spine had prickled with guilt then. He should join the search. His neighbors, the Sampsons, Neil and his two teenage sons, were all out on their horses, looking for her. They were all meeting in the small town of Dandang, a few miles west of his farm, if what Dusty heard on his radio was correct. Surely there were enough people out hunting for her. He didn't need to join their ranks. And he needed to get those sheep down from the higher grazing paddock, right now. Shaking his head, he'd hopped back on his motorbike and set off to round up more sheep.

He'd emptied two of the three higher paddocks and got most of his sheep safely into the holding paddock before that prickling sensation had become so hot he could no longer stand it. Something was telling him to go and saddle Scout. For some reason, some stupid unknown, bloody sissy reason he couldn't explain, and would never admit to another living soul, he felt a pull towards the mountain. Almost as if he knew she was up there. His eyes roamed over the imposing figure of Mount Jagungle, rising up from his back fence. The SES were concentrating the search on the western side of the mountain, because that's where she told her uncle she was going. So why did his gaze keep returning to a ridge half-way up on the eastern side, nearest him? It was bloody stupid. But the more he tried to ignore the feeling, the hotter the back of his neck burned, as if there was a fishhook stuck in the middle of his chest, tugging gently until he had no choice but to whistle up Scout from the horse yard and saddle the young gelding.

'Are you still there, Dusty? Over.' The radio crackled to life again, as Dusty steered Scout around a large stand of snow gums.

Pulling the hand-held radio out of his shirt pocket, he said,

'Yes, John. Go ahead. Over.'

'How far out are you from Kidman's hut? Over.'

'Probably another twenty minutes. Over.' Dusty cast his gaze to the darkening sky and crossed his fingers. Hopefully the quickly fading light would last that long. It was just after 4 pm, but the smudged grey clouds, heavy with their load of snow had sucked the last of the afternoon sunlight from the day, turning everything dark and gloomy.

'We're not sure if a team can get up to you tonight. This weather is coming in fast. They're predicting a blizzard. Over' *Great.* The absolute last thing he needed. His thoughts went back to the small group of sheep he hadn't managed to bring down to the safety of the farmhouse. If he lost his precious sheep because of this woman, he'd ... He left the thought unfinished. Of course, if came to a choice between a human life and that of his sheep, he'd choose her. But it was a close thing.

With a heavy sigh he replied, 'Thanks for the heads up. We should be okay once we reach the hut. I'll treat her for hypothermia and get some fluids into her. Let me know as soon as someone can get to us. Over.'

'Will do, Dusty. Good luck. Over and Out.'

'Yeah, thanks,' Dusty muttered to himself. Ehlana stirred in front of him, shifting slightly in the saddle, as if the radio conversation had gotten through some of the fog of hypothermia and dehydration. He clasped her tighter around the middle and hunched his shoulders against the cold wind that cut through his thick wool sweater. How had she survived out here all night without a coat? She must be stronger than she looked, because he was definitely feeling the cold now he'd forfeited his coat to her.

'Come on, Scout,' he clucked encouragingly. 'Let's go.' The plucky appaloosa quickened his pace up the steep, sloping ground, picking his way through the thick scrub towards the ridge above them and the safety of the little wooden hut, while thunder boomed around them and the temperature dropped even lower.

Lana

Why couldn't she open her eyes? Her eyelids had been glued shut. It was the only explanation. Or else someone had placed a heavy weight on her face.

Lana tried again. At first each lid refused to budge. But then slowly, ever so slowly, her left one parted just a crack. Then her right also opened. She blinked and blinked, but everything was fuzzy and dim. Someone was lifting her, her body cradled inside strong arms, her head resting against a solid chest. It was a man. He smelled like fresh cut grass and earth and warmth. The strong arms laid her gently onto a wooden surface, her head cradled softly in his palm. Then he was gone and she was left alone. Panic set in.

She tried to speak. 'Hello? Where am I?' The words sounded muttered and blurry inside her head and she wasn't even sure she'd said them out loud.

She tried again. 'Where am I? Who are you?' This time she'd definitely said the words, but it was as if she were speaking through a fluffy cotton sheet. She tried to move, to roll onto her side, but her muscles were slow to respond, like she was moving through molasses.

'What happened?' she asked. Why couldn't she remember where she was? The last thing she recollected clearly was arriving at her aunt and uncle's house in her sleek white sedan, gliding up the steep drive and watching the familiar tall trees close in around her. Tom, her uncle, had stood on the verandah, arms open in welcome. She'd returned his hug, enjoying the smell of his damp, slightly smoky sweater as he wrapped her up. But that was days ago. Wasn't it?

A dark form loomed over her and she wanted to scream, but the fuzziness in her head made her reaction slow and it came out as a croak.

'You're okay,' said a deep voice. 'We're in Kidman's hut. I'm going to get you dry and warm. You've got hypothermia.' A face appeared in front of hers suddenly, as the man knelt down beside her.

'Wh—what? How—how did I get here?' So many questions crowded her brain, but not many of them made any sense.

'You went for a horse ride and got lost. Don't you remember?' His voice was deep, but she could sense an undercurrent of impatience. 'Don't worry, I'll tell you all about it soon, but my first priority is to get you warm. To get us both warm. Okay?' The weight of his hand landed on her shoulder, and he stared at her with kind brown eyes. Brown, like rich, dark chocolate. Deep and swirling. She just nodded.

He handed her a bottle of water, breaking the seal on the top as he did so. 'Take small sips of this. Sorry, I don't have anything warmer at the moment, but you need to re-hydrate as well as get warm. Okay?' Again, she just nodded, but accepted the bottle of water.

That's when she noticed she was wearing an overlarge, bulky coat. His coat? Probably. And there was something warm and soft on her head. A knit cap. He must've put that there too, because she was pretty sure she wasn't wearing a knit cap beforehand. She pulled the coat tighter around herself. It was hard even to do that simple task. She'd been out riding and got lost? Why couldn't she remember that?

Her bones felt limp and spongy, her muscles like water. She tried to wiggle her toes inside her boots. They responded, but slowly, sluggishly. Some part of Lana understood she was cold, deathly cold, but for now she didn't feel cold, she just felt sleepy. Lethargic. Like swimming through wet cement. Wouldn't it just be easier to close her eyes and …

'Hey, stay with me, Ehlana.' His deep voice was back again, and something heavy and soft landed on top of her. Blankets. He started to wrap them around her, tucking the edges in like she was a child.

'Lana,' she croaked.

'What?' His big hands stopped moving.

'Call me Lana. I hate Ehlana.'

He gave a grunt. Whether it was in humor or acknowledgement, she wasn't sure. 'I'm Dusty,' he said and then he was gone again and she could hear noises somewhere close by. Where had he said they were? In some kind of hut? She tried to lift her head. Her neck wouldn't obey, but she managed to swivel her shoulders just enough so the man, Dusty, came into view.

It took a few moments for her eyes to adjust to the dim light inside the hut. Over in the corner, Dusty was crouched in front of a large, stone fireplace. The sound of snapping branches filled the small space and then his hand reached out and placed a pile of kindling in the centre of the fireplace. She watched the muscles of his broad shoulders flex and bulge beneath his thick woolen sweater as he moved.

Her eyes roved over the interior of the hut. It was basic. A roughly hewn wooden floor, with walls to match. A simple wooden table was anchored to the floor in one corner next to the fireplace, and two large metal storage trunks leaned up against the far wall, one with the lid thrown open. A bench, a couple of feet off the floor, also made of bare wood, lined the last wall and extended around the corner to blend with the bench she was lying on. A very simple form of a bed, she assumed.

A match flared in the gloom and suddenly welcoming flames danced in the fireplace. A fire would be nice, Lana thought absentmindedly. Perhaps it might warm her up a bit. She stared at the flickering flames, hypnotized.

Dusty came back to her side after a few minutes.

'Thank God they keep this place well-stocked with wood and matches. That fire is going to warm us up in no time. I'm just going to check on my horse. I won't be long, I promise. Don't go anywhere.' She would've laughed out loud if her numb lips allowed. Instead she just grunted.

But true to his word, within a few minutes she heard the wooden door clang shut as a blast of freezing air swirled in on the man's heels.

Her gaze traced his pathway across the small hut to the fireplace, where he dropped an armload of wood on the floor, then added some more, larger logs to the flames.

'Right, let's get you more comfortable,' he said, looming over her again. What did he mean by that? 'Can you sit up for a moment?' She very much doubted it, but he got a hand under her shoulders and levered her up without really waiting for her answer. She had to lean her shoulders up against the wall, but she actually made a pretty good job of staying upright.

'I know this might sound odd, but I need to get some of those clothes off you.'

'You're going to do what?' she asked, hoping her voice sounded as scornful as she felt. Instead it came out croaky and wretched.

'Your clothes are wet. In order to get you warm, I need to get your wet clothes off and wrap you in some dry blankets.' Oh, okay then. That sounded a little more logical. 'And then I'm going to get under the blankets with you. Body heat is the quickest way to warm someone up.' Did she just hear him right? Was he going to hop in bed with her?

'It's basic first aid. You should know that.'

She just stared at him as if he were mad. Finally he shrugged and bent down to remove his boots, tugging hers off as well, and then her sodden socks too. She wasn't sure what to think or what to do. When her bare toes hit the wooden floor, she hardly felt it. They were like chunks of ice, unresponsive and leaden. Perhaps he was right, perhaps she did need a little warming up.

Dusty pulled a few more blankets off the floor and spread them over the bench to make the hard wood more comfortable. In a swift movement that Lana almost missed, he tugged his sweater over his head. Followed by his red flannelette shirt. Which left him with just a ribbed white singlet stretched over a very impressive set of pecs. Even in her confusion and cold-induced stupor, Lana could appreciate just how nice a chest the man had. Broad, muscular, toned, with a sprinkling of dark curling hair. Then he undid the buttons on his blue jeans.

Oh hell. He was really going to do this.

His jeans landed on the floor with a soft thud and she was staring a pair of powerful thighs, topped off by black briefs that hugged every contour. Lana swallowed hard. Those thighs definitely matched his chest.

He leant towards her and tried to gently unwrap his coat from around her shoulders, but her fingers tightened instinctively on the folds.

'It's alright, I promise I'm not an axe murderer.' That impatience was back in his tone again, and it made her angry. He had no right to be impatient with her. Did he? She wished she could remember exactly what'd happened. Was she to blame for their predicament? Obviously, she'd been out in the bush all night. On her own. In the freezing cold. And he'd found her. And now she was suffering from hypothermia. Well at least that's what he was telling her.

'I promise this is all strictly business. I'm not going to molest you.' Damn straight he wasn't. She wasn't the type of girl to let a strange man anywhere near her. Well, not under normal circumstances anyway. But these definitely weren't normal circumstances.

'Are you going to sit there all night and let me freeze out here? Or are you going to get on with it and let me help you?' She could tell it took some effort to keep his voice under control. There was a temper there, boiling just below the surface. And he was probably right, she was being silly. He did look very alive and warm, standing there in front of her.

With a grunt she unwrapped the heavy coat from around her, then tried to pull her sweater over her head, but her numb fingers wouldn't obey.

'Let me do it,' he said and started to remove her garment. She had a thin cotton t-shirt on underneath. He wasn't going to take that off as well, was he? But no, he left that on, and started to help her off with her black skinny jeans. They were still damp and clung stubbornly to her cold skin, making it hard to get them off. Dusty turned and hung her clothes over a makeshift line he'd strung across one corner of the hut so they would dry. And there she was, sitting in her underwear and t-shirt. At least she still had the knit cap on.

A memory came to her, of her uncle Tom, telling her to put on one of his work coats hanging by the back door. They were warm and scratchy and smelled like dust and sunshine. But she'd kept walking to the stables and ignored him. That's right, it was coming back to her now. She'd taken one of her uncle's horses, Nomad, out for a ride. It was only going to be a quick ride, half an hour at the most, she'd yelled back at him. An hour tops. Her own sweater was warm enough, it was a snug—and very expensive—lambswool turtleneck.

And it hadn't been that cold yesterday morning. But then it often got warmer just before a really cold front moved in, almost as if Mother Nature was lulling the unwary into a false sense of security. Silly. She'd been so silly. But she thought she knew better. Why did she never listen?

As she sat there, the cold air engulfed her bare skin and she started to shiver.

'Lie down,' he commanded. He rolled the coat up and placed it at one end to form a makeshift pillow. She lay down on the raspy woolen blankets and he climbed in beside her, shuffling over until his long legs lay close to hers, pulling her into his chest as if she were a rag doll, then layering more and more blankets over the top of them. Her teeth chattered uncontrollably now.

'Don't worry, the shivering is a good sign. It means you're warming up.'

'Oh, r—really?' She could hardly speak through her chattering teeth.

'I'm actually not sure,' he replied with a gruff laugh. 'But it sounded good, huh?'

It was the first time she'd heard him laugh. It was a nice sound. It reverberated through his chest and into her bones.

'Now let's get you warm.' He tugged her harder in against his chest and wrapped his long, lean legs around her. It felt so good. Heat radiated off his body like he was her own personal hot water bottle, and she found herself snuggling in as close as she could get.

It should've been awkward, entangled beneath the blankets with a strange man in a tiny hut in the middle of absolutely nowhere. But it wasn't. In fact, it almost felt … good.

Dusty

The only sound inside the hut was the occasional crackle from the fire. Outside the wind howled like a savage beast. The storm was finally here, and it was smashing into the mountain-side with a fierce vengeance. John had been right when he said the SES team wouldn't make it up here. No living thing should be out on a night like tonight. Thank God he'd found her when he did. She might not have survived another night out here alone. A guilty shiver ran through him at the thought he'd nearly put his sheep ahead of rescuing this woman.

Dusty still wasn't sure what it was that'd brought him up the mountain. All of the SES's information said Lana should never have got this far on her little horse. The rescue units had been combing the lower ridges of the mountain, over on the other side, near the town of Dandang. They'd never have made it around to this zone in time. But something had called him out here. Something … He let the thought drop. It'd do no good to start considering all that paranormal shit. He didn't believe in it, anyway.

The girl's shivering seemed to be subsiding.

'Is your h—horse going to be o—okay,' she asked suddenly, her voice breaking through the silence.

'Scout will be fine. There's a small wood shed out the back.

I cleaned it up a little and put him in there. At least he'll be dry and out of the worst of the weather.'

'Oh, that's g—good.' The relief in her voice was palpable. It was sweet she was worried about his horse. Considering she was the one who'd nearly frozen to death.

"Oh God. Nomad. What about N—Nomad? Do you know what happened t—to my horse?' She couldn't get the words out quick enough.

'He's fine. He arrived back at your uncle's farm last night. He wasn't stupid enough to spend the night out in the freezing cold.' Dusty laughed. 'You must've fallen off him somehow. Do you remember?'

'I'm not sure.' She sounded deep in thought, as if trying to dredge up some kind of memory.

'It's okay if you don't. Hypothermia will do that to you.'

He wanted to let her know it was fine, it'd come back eventually, and was about to say so when she started to speak in a low voice. 'I remember I went the opposite way t—to what I told Tom.' He grunted in reply. He figured. It *was* stupid thing to do, but he was gentlemanly enough not to say it out loud. 'I was only going to ride out to the c—clump of tall scribbly gums on the ridge above the farm. To get a few ideas for my next p—painting. Those trees have amazing patterns on their bark. But t—then I had this sudden urge to turn right instead, to go up to this little clearing I'd been to once with Tom. It's such a beautiful view from up there.' She stopped talking, perhaps thinking it hadn't been such a good idea after all.

'But you got lost,' he volunteered into the sudden silence.

'Yeah, kind of.' She shrugged her shoulder into his chest. 'I followed a trail, but I think it took us too far up the mountain.'

'And then what?' He kept his voice probing but gentle.

'I think I must've started to feel a little nervous, because

Nomad got jumpy all of a sudden.'

'That can happen. They're intelligent creatures. They understand more than you think, you can transmit your fear into the horse if you're not careful.'

'Yeah well, a big kangaroo suddenly appeared out of the undergrowth and then it took off at the sight of us. Because Nomad was already kind of spooked he shied and then reared.'

'And you fell off?'

'I didn't hurt myself though. I just kind of landed on my bum on a pile of soft tussocks and got the wind knocked out of me. But Nomad took off like he'd seen a ghost.'

'He probably thought he had,' laughed Dusty. 'Poor horse, you can't really blame him.'

'Oh, I don't. It was all my fault. Oh my, Joyce and Tom must've been worried sick about me.' She started to sit up at the thought of the agonizing time she'd put her aunt and uncle through last night.

'It's fine, John from HQ will have told them I found you by now. Don't worry. And I'm not sure you should take all the blame, either.' He gave a low chuckle. 'Shit happens. Sometimes it just isn't your day. You have to take the good with the bad.'

He hoped his philosophical outlook on life might sooth her guilty conscience. Everything had turned out okay in the end. Her family would just be feeling relieved right now she'd been found alive. Perhaps there might be recriminations later, but for now they were probably rejoicing. And sometimes, shit did happen and there wasn't a lot you could do about it.

The silence settled in around them once more. It should've been awkward, this silence between two strangers. Two strangers who were right at this moment, closer than most people ever got. Intimate. That's how it felt, with both of them curled around each other. Intimate. But not awkward.

Strange really.

He'd been right, she was tiny. Especially compared to his large frame. Her thin arms and slim torso felt almost fragile in his embrace. It was like hugging a block of ice, however. A human shaped block of ice. But that ice was slowly thawing around the edges. Her hands and feet were still chilled, but he could feel the heat returning to her chest, see the color slowly returning to her face. A face that lay mere inches away from his own. Dwarfed by his large grey knit cap he'd shoved on her head, it made her look almost elfin.

The most startling thing he noticed about her, as she nestled into the crook of his arm, was the nose ring. One of those rings that pierced the middle of the septum, hung down like a mini bull-ring. He'd always thought of those women who wore nose rings as alternative, unconventional, dropouts, but she didn't strike him as any of those things. On Lana it made her seem even more fragile ... But also free-spirited somehow.

She was young, too. Her face fresh and unlined. Unlike his own, which had seen too much sun and wind.

'How old are you?' The question popped out before he could censure it.

'What?'

'Sorry, you don't have to answer that, it was rude,' he said with a grimace. He was really rusty at this kind of thing. He hadn't had much practice talking to a woman in a while now. At least not since his mum was diagnosed with cancer. Since he'd become her full-time carer.

'Oh. I'm twenty-three. Why? How old are you?'

Shit, now he owed her an answer.

'I'm twenty-nine.' Her shivering had almost completely stopped now. That was a good thing. He'd get up and make them both a hot cup of tea soon. Warm fluids were supposed to be good for hypothermia patients. Thankfully this hut had recently been re-stocked with provisions for winter. The local community, along with National Parks and Wildlife had done a good job restoring these old huts scattered throughout the Snowy Mountains. They were kept stocked with the basics for just this kind of emergency. Lost hikers or farmers caught out by a fast-moving storm.

'Not that much older than me,' she said quietly. 'What do you do? Are you a farmer?'

'Yes. I run sheep and alpacas. How did you guess?' She wouldn't be able to see his sardonic grin, because his chin was resting on the top of her cap-clad head, but she caught his tone.

'It was the boots. The boots are always a dead give-away,' she jibed. 'I know a little bit about the country. I come up and visit my aunt and uncle, Joyce and Tom Fanning, nearly every month. To get away from the city for a few days. Do you know them?'

'Yep, they're down the road a bit from me. I know Tom from the Volunteer Rural Fire Service. Nice bloke. Can't say I know your aunt that well. Talked to her a few times at the Country Women's Association fetes and other functions around town. She brought food over a couple of times when my mum was sick. Just before she died.'

Damn, why had he said that? Now she was going to ask questions about his mum. He didn't like questions. They opened old wounds. People were always trying to get him to talk about things he'd rather forget. Unconsciously his shoulders tightened and his lips thinned into a severe line. Waiting for the inevitable.

'Ah, that sounds like Joyce.' When she didn't say anything more, a pang of contrition twisted through him. She seemed to understand he wouldn't welcome her prying. Perhaps he'd misjudged her. He seemed to be doing that a lot with this girl. Or perhaps it was just she was good at surprising him.

The wind dropped a little in ferocity outside and they both lay listening to the branches of the nearby tree bang indignantly on the corrugated iron roof above.

'This storm is bad, huh?'

'Yeah, it's a pretty bad one. We always get at least one or two like this each year. This one's a little late in the season, that's all.'

'I'm glad I'm not still outside.'

'Me too,' he agreed. They left the rest unsaid. He sent up a silent prayer of thanks to whoever was listening that he'd found her in time. A sound like galloping horses suddenly erupted overhead, as sheets of rain began to lash the tiny hut.

'Wow, that's some incredible rain.' He almost didn't catch her comment over the thundering downpour. They lay together and listened to the rain pound onto the tin roof, as if Mother Nature was intent on drowning them both. After a few minutes the rain ran out of fury and the pounding diminished, turned into a more regular, consistent patter on the iron sheeting. Familiar and rhythmic. It was a peaceful sound. It reminded him of days spent inside, safe and cocooned and soothed as nature replenished the earth. As a kid there was nothing he loved better than to huddle into the window seat in the living room, with a book about fierce dragons and courageous knights, contemplating the furious weather lash down outside, while he watched and read.

'There's nothing like the sound of rain on a tin roof, is there?' Lana said into his chest. He grunted in consternation. Another unusual sentiment, coming from a city-girl.

'Nope, it's the best sound in the world,' he agreed. And it was. Dusty always stopped to listen to the rain on the roof wherever he was, whatever he was doing. It evoked emotions of happier times, reminded him how lucky he was to be living in the country, not caged and cramped by a job in the city.

'Especially when we're warm and dry inside,' she added. 'Well, definitely dry. And getting warmer by the minute.' She wriggled against him, trying to get closer, if that were possible.

Hah, she had a sense of humor as well. It made him curious about her.

'Your turn now. You know I'm a farmer. What do you do for a living?' Her back stiffened beneath his hands ever so slightly.

'I'm a project manager.' From the tone of her voice, it sounded like he'd hit a nerve. Defensive about her job, perhaps? Interesting.

'What exactly does that mean. And don't say you manage projects.' He felt her smile beneath his chin, some of the wariness leaving her.

'You took the words right out of my mouth. I do manage projects,' she laughed. 'But if you want to know the details, I work for an architectural firm.'

'Wow, that's ... um, interesting.' He was surprised. Not at all what he'd been expecting her to say. 'Don't take this the wrong way, but aren't you young to be taking on that kind of responsibility?'

'I don't know, am I? My dad owns the company. He was the one who suggested I do the degree at uni. He promised me a job once I finished. I only graduated six months ago. But it's okay. I'm learning the ropes. Learning how to deal with client expectations, keep the engineers and contractors happy. The site visits are the most interesting part of the job so far. At least they get me out of the office.'

'Ah, I see.' A picture was staring to form in his head. He knew from experience that family expectations could weigh heavily on a person's shoulders. From the underlying tone she was trying desperately to keep out of her voice, it was clear this wasn't her first choice. And it was also clear there was friction between her and her father.

'Are you good at what you do?'

'Not if you listen to my dad,' she snorted, but then seemed to regret her hasty words, and added, 'But I think I do okay. I get on well with most of the clients. And even though Dad's only giving me the smaller projects to deal with right now, I've never failed to finish one on time.'

That wasn't really what he wanted to know. 'Okay, let me rephrase that. Do you like what you do?'

'Of course I do.' Her back stiffened again. 'It's a job, it earns me money, and I'm pretty good at it. Why? Do you like what you do?' Her voice rose an octave as she asked the question and he thought it might be time to back off this conversation. He hadn't intended for her to get all defensive.

'Sure. I love living on the farm. It's a hard slog sometimes, but I wouldn't change it for anything.' It was the truth. He couldn't imagine himself living in a town house in the city, with no open paddocks, or the beauty of the mountains to fill his view. Locked away at some desk job in a giant high-rise building. Not any more, anyway. When he'd been young and naive, he'd wanted to live in the city. Moved to Sydney to do a degree in engineering. But then seven years ago the accident happened. The day after a wild storm, much like this one, his dad had been out clearing felled trees. They all knew the dangers of driving the old tractor around their hilly property. His dad should've been more careful. Perhaps he'd become too blasé after so long working the land, had often bragged he could find his way around the farm blindfolded. The tractor had slipped down a boggy hillside and rolled. His dad was killed instantly, or at least that's what the paramedics told him afterwards. And Dusty hadn't even thought twice about what needed to be done. His mum couldn't cope alone on the farm. So he gave up his lucrative dream job and moved back to the mountains.

There had been three or four good years, with him and his mum working side by side. She'd started a side-business, breeding alpacas, which had started to bring in almost as much money as the sheep. But then she'd got sick. Cancer. She'd died almost two years ago to the day.

And now he was running the farm on his own. Alone. The word lonely never really entered his mind. He was always so busy, he never had time to think about his circumstances. Just got on with what needed to be done. Loneliness was for the old or the weak.

'Have you got any brothers or sisters?' Perhaps if he changed the topic slightly, she might not get quite so defensive.

'Yes, a younger sister, Gail. She's still at uni. Studying to be a geologist of all things.' It worked. The offended tone disappeared. Replaced by something akin to tenderness. Whatever misgivings she had about her father, they obviously didn't extend to her sister.

'What about you?'

'I did have a younger brother, but he died when he was a year old. Pneumonia I think. I was only three at the time. My parents never had any more kids after that.'

'Oh, I'm sorry.'

'No need to be, I don't really remember him.' The rain still pattered away on the tin roof, filling the hut with the satisfying sound. A log collapsed in a flare of sparks on the fire. He needed to get up and put some more wood on it. Soon. He'd do it soon. Just a few more minutes beneath the blankets with Lana. To make sure she was completely warm. Out of danger. He didn't want to admit it, but it was nice, lying here. Talking. Finding out about each other. Feeling her body next to his.

'I also like to paint. I have a studio here at my aunt and uncle's place. Whenever I'm not working, I pai—' Lana stopped talking abruptly and he got the distinct impression she'd said more than she intended.

Perhaps now the truth was coming out. Had Lana just revealed her true passion? It certainly rang truer than her exaggeration that she loved working for her father.

'That sounds like lots more fun that being shackled to a desk all day,' he prompted lightly.

'Yes, well, perhaps it is, but it'll never pay the bills. So it's more of a whimsical fancy than anything substantial.'

Dusty was sure those words were more her father's than Lana's, but he kept his thoughts to himself.

'Tom lets me use a corner of his work shed to keep all my gear in, so I can paint whenever I come to stay. It's so beautiful up here, so inspiring.' Her voice took on a dreamy edge and he imagined her eyes might have taken on a faraway gleam.

'It was Tom who encouraged me to keep painting. Ever since I was a young girl, I can always remember Tom talking about how much he loved my drawings. How he thought I would become world-renowned one day.' Lana gave a quiet snort. 'And when my dad told me to stop living in a dream and give up my painting, get on with reality, it was Tom who stood up for me. Who told my dad he didn't know what he was talking about. Thank God he's so different to his brother.'

It sounded like Tom was perhaps more of a father-figure to Lana than her own dad, but Dusty didn't voice that thought either. Instead, he asked, 'Are you self-taught then?' It didn't sound like she would've had enough time around her uni degree to take art classes as well.

'Yes, I am. I've just always wanted to draw. Always known how to paint. It's kind of like an instinct. How did you know?'

'Just a lucky guess.' He gave a shrug. It didn't surprise him, this girl had an idealistic look in her eyes that hinted at her artistic ability. What did surprise him was she continued to slog away at a job she obviously hated in the city. Just to please her father.

'I'd love to see your paintings someday. If you'll let me.' He was suddenly intrigued to know what kind of pictures she created. If he saw them, would they give him a little more insight into the real Lana, perhaps?

'Oh, really? I don't let many people see my paintings. But you can come over one day if you like.' For the first time since he'd gotten under the blankets with her, she tipped her head upwards, so she could look at him. Her eyes reflected the orange glow of the firelight. Light blue, the color of a sky on a winter's morning. The nose ring also sparkled in the flames, reminding him he hardly knew this captivating girl. So different from anyone else he'd met. And all of a sudden he found himself wanting to get to know her. To delve deeper into her. Thank God he'd joined the search. Thank God he'd found her. All of that earlier irritation towards her vanished now.

'I can't wait,' he replied a little gruffly. 'Now, I need to get up and see to the fire and make you a drink.'

'What?' She jumped like a startled rabbit in his arms. 'Why? I'm fine. You don't need to get up.' Dusty suppressed a chuckle. It seemed she didn't want him to leave almost as much as he didn't want to go.

Lana

'Can you hear that?' Dusty asked.

'What?' Lana tipped her head on the side. 'It's stopped raining, is that what you mean?' She cradled the hot cup of sweet tea in her hands, the warmth seeping right through to her bones. He was right, she needed the drink, it was doing her good. Dusty made her sit up on their makeshift bed, still swathed in blankets and offered her the metal mug filled with the warming beverage. Now he was banging around near the fireplace, heating up some tinned baked beans for them both to eat.

'Yes, it's stopped raining. But do you know why?'

Lana just shook her head and stared at him in anticipation. Then he did something completely unexpected. He strode over and flung the door wide open. It was pitch black outside. It was scary at how completely and utterly dark it was out there. The glow from the now blazing fire cast a small pool of light just outside the doorway. And in that light she finally made out what Dusty meant. Small white flakes drifted weightlessly down to earth.

'Snow? Is it snowing?' And now she knew what to listen for, she could indeed hear the snow falling. A sound as soft as cat paws padding across the roof. A gentle whispering against the corrugated iron.

'Yes it is,' Dusty declared as he shut the door again before all the warm air could leak out. He'd put his flannelette shirt and jeans back on when he'd jumped out of bed to stoke the fire and put the pot on to boil. Lana let out a quiet sigh as he put his clothes back on. She'd rather been enjoying the view of his powerful thighs and straight, muscled back. Especially now she knew them intimately. Enjoyed having her arms wrapped around those shoulders, and her legs entwined with his. She now knew exactly how solid and warm his chest was; her head had been cradled against it for the past few hours, her ear resting just above his heart. And she also appreciated just how impressive his biceps were as they'd curled behind her head and across her stomach, keeping her warm and safe.

Dusty was a splendid looking man. There was no denying it. A thick shock of black hair covered his head. A few tufts of which were now standing up at odd angles from where he'd used his coat as a pillow. But it just made him even more endearing.

She now saw through his gruff demeanor, which'd scared her back when he'd first ordered her to take her clothes off and get under the blankets. Now she understood the big-hearted, contemplative man that lay beneath. She knew enough of the farmers who lived up here in the Snowies from visiting her uncle over the years. Typical of most alpine men, Dusty was steady as a rock, laconic, hard-working and shaped by the elements. But that was where the similarities stopped. There was a certain sadness that radiated from Dusty. She wasn't sure if it was loneliness—if she'd caught his words earlier, his mum had died a while ago and he had no one else helping him on the farm now—or perhaps it was just he was more introspective than most. Obviously highly intelligent and aware of everything around him. She was tantalized. By that spark of … whatever it was inside him. As well as by that awesome body he'd now covered up. She blew on her tea again and wondered how she could get him to take his clothes off and come back to the blankets with her.

'Have you finished that tea yet?' Reflexively she took another gulp, hoping she hadn't been caught staring.

'Nearly,' she replied.

'Well, the beans are just about ready.' He turned his back again and she continued her perusal. Unique. That's what he was. More robust. More alive than any other man she'd met. He made her feel safe, somehow. And she didn't think it was just because he'd rescued her from nearly freezing to death on the mountain-side. It was more than that. As if he could see beneath her shields, down to the real woman who lurked below. Down to the Lana not even her father or sister understood.

How could she be thinking this way? She hardly knew the man. Just because they'd lain together, body against body, for two hours, didn't mean she knew him at all.

'Here you go.' He handed her a tin plate piled high with the beans. The steam wafted up to her nose and her stomach growled loudly. She dug in with the battered metal spoon he'd given her and was surprised when she next looked down to find her plate empty.

Dusty chuckled from across the room, where he was eating his own plateful standing up. 'Hungry much?'

'Just a little,' she admitted.

'I'll make you some more later. The fire should be right for a while. Perhaps we should try and get some sleep. The rescue team won't be here till morning. How are you feeling? Better?'

'Yes, much better. Almost human. Thanks to you.' She cast him a shy glance and he gave her a quick, awkward smile in return. It was charming, the way he was so humble. Didn't want to take any credit for rescuing her.

'Move over then.' His fingers found the hem of his shirt

and pulled it over his head.

Her prayers were answered. He was coming back to bed. She put the empty plate on the floor and scooted over next to the wall, so there was room for him to join her on the wooden platform.

His big arms surrounded her and she couldn't help the sigh that escaped her lips. It felt so right, to be back in his arms like this. Both of them lying and listening to the snow fall quietly all around them.

'Are you sleepy?' he asked, the sound rumbling through his chest and into her ear.

'Not too bad. You?'

'Yeah, I am. I've had a rough couple of days. I should really stay awake and make sure you're okay, though.'

'I'm fine,' she said indignantly.

'Yeah, you do seem pretty fine to me.'

Her heart did a little skip in her chest. Should she read anything into that last comment? There was definitely a double meaning there if she wanted to think about it.

'Tell me more about yourself,' he said, stifling a yawn.

'Not much to tell, really. It's just me and Gail and my dad. My mum left us a long time ago. She's living in Brazil, I think.'

'Mmm hmm. Go on.' Again, the reverberation of his voice buzzed through her ear. She liked the sound. Then his hand started to absently stroke up and down her back. A soft flash of his fingertips over the ridges of her spine. Distracting her. Did he know what he was doing to her? She had to physically pull her mind back from the places it was wandering as those fingers traced lazily over her back. What'd she been talking about before? Her family, that's right.

'I like to come up and visit Tom and Joyce as often as I can. Just to get away, you know.' She loved escaping up here. It was a long drive from Sydney, but it was worth it, and she tried to come every month or so. Thank God her uncle was nothing like her father. Tom and Joyce never had children. Lana never really knew why. Probably because they couldn't conceive for some reason. Her aunt and uncle loved kids and were so warm and giving. There was no doubt in her mind they would've had children if they could. Which was perhaps why they were so pleased whenever she visited. Treated her more like a daughter than a niece. And in some ways she treated them more like her parents than perhaps she should. Especially after her mum just up and left the day after she graduated from high school. Said she couldn't put up with their father for another day longer. And Lana didn't really blame her. After all, she should've been old enough not to need her mother then, but it still hurt. And Joyce seemed to understand that. And Tom accepted her for what she was. Encouraged her painting. Had even spent a day with her, cleaning out a corner of his large shed, helping her erect an easel and set up her paints and canvasses. There was a big window through which she had a perfect view of Mount Jagungle and the Snowy Mountains beyond. Joyce kept telling her how fantastic an artist she was and how beautiful her paintings were. She'd even said she had a friend who was a gallery director for a small but prestigious gallery in the nearby town of Cooma, who'd take a look at her paintings, if she ever wanted to show them. But Lana never really believed either of them, not really. She wasn't good enough. It was always just a hobby to her.

Lana used acrylics on canvas. Big, bold canvasses that filled the whole corner of the shed. Her paintings were of the mountains and the leaves on the trees, the brilliant, overarching sky, and the dark rivers and streams bisecting the hills. Joyce said they were vibrant, full of life and color. That they lifted her soul and inspired her, made her happy and sad all at the same time. But Lana had never shown her artwork to anyone else. Yes, it made her satisfied and filled a craving deep within. But that's all it really was, just a sideline, a diversion.

'If you love it so much, why don't you just come and live up here? Chuck that desk job in the city and come and do what you want to instead.' Dusty's voice was thick with sleep and his last words were mumbled, so Lana almost missed them.

'Ha,' she laughed softly. 'What I wouldn't give for that dream to become reality.' She didn't add her father would never allow it. Not in a million years. She'd never hear the end of his tirades as to how he'd paid for her uni degree and how she owed him now. Sometimes she wished she hadn't done that damned degree. Wished her father didn't believe he owned her soul. Besides the job and her dad's expectations, she had bills to pay, commitments in the city, a life to lead. She couldn't just drop all that and leave. And Gail lived in the city, she couldn't abandon her sister, she needed her. Didn't she?

Dusty's breathing had become slow and even. He'd fallen asleep. Poor man was probably exhausted. Working on the farm by himself, then out searching for her sorry ass most of the day. She took the opportunity to lever herself up onto one elbow and stare down at his face, mapping the contours of his square jaw and high cheekbones in the firelight. He was stunning, and it made her heart yearn for something she never even knew she wanted until this very moment.

How different would her life be if she'd chosen another path? What if she did live up here, in these beautiful mountains? What if she was free to paint every day? Would people really buy her paintings, as Joyce was sure they would?

Laying her head back down on Dusty's chest, she closed her eyes and listened to his steady breathing mingling with the falling snow. It was surreal, being out here in a tiny hut in the middle of the dark foreboding mountains, in the arms of a man who'd just saved her life. A wonderful, but lonely man.

There was a lot for Lana to think about as she breathed the solitude in and out, in and out.

Dusty

Grey morning light slanted in through the small window above Dusty's head. He had no idea what time it was. He went to roll over to check if the fire was still alight, but a weight on his chest stopped him.

Lana. She was still asleep, using him as a pillow. He'd drifted to sleep last night listening to Lana talk about her family, and her love of painting. It soothed him and it was one of the best night's sleep he'd had in a long time. Slept like a log, he had. Often, Dusty found himself prowling around his cold old house in the dead of the night, unable to sleep because his mind was buzzing with millions of worries, debts that needed to be paid, how he was going to afford to keep feeding his mother's beloved alpacas, wool prices, meat prices, the fact his threadbare carpet needed replacing. But none of those things bothered him last night. Not when there was a lithe, warm body snuggled next to his.

He looked down and saw the top of her head, her brown hair all tousled and messy. Very cute. The knit cap must've come off sometime in the night. He could feel the rest of her was warm as toast beneath the blankets. The curve of her soft cheek was the only part of her face visible from his vantage point. It had a healthy pink tinge. How would that delicate skin feel beneath his fingertip?

What was he thinking?

He'd done his job. She was safe and over the worst of the hypothermia. Now he needed to get up and get them ready, before the SES team arrived. Except he didn't want to move. Not yet. Didn't want to wake her.

But he was too late. Lana stirred and then stretched just like a cat, toes pointed and back arched.

'Is it morning?' she mumbled into his chest.

'Yep. Time to get up.'

'Do we have to? I like it right here.' That's when she tipped her head up and back, using his bicep for support, so she could stare him straight in the face. His heart stopped beating when those blue eyes collided with his.

So do I. That's what he wanted to say, but the words wouldn't leave his throat.

'I can't believe how well I slept,' she said. 'I never knew a hard, wooden bench could be so comfortable. It must be the pillow I'm using,' she added with a cheeky grin.

For once, all of his witty repartee seemed to have deserted him and he couldn't form a reply. Instead he was ensnared by those beautiful eyes of hers. He couldn't look away.

Her face turned serious as she took in his unwavering stare, and her gaze flicked to his lips and then back up to his eyes. What was she thinking?

'I haven't thanked you yet. For saving me.'

'You don't ne—' The rest of his words disappeared as her lips found his. Supple and light, she landed soft as a snowflake. And he let her kiss him, invited her in. She tasted sleepy and warm and wanting. Like a promise. He craved more of her. Her lips set off a fire in his belly. Of its own accord one of his hands came up to cup the back of her neck and he pulled her in for more. Deeper, harder, their mouths meshed as one and she responded to his need with equal intensity. She moved then, climbed on top of him and lay along his body, his other hand coming up to curve around her buttock.

'Mmm,' she groaned deep in her throat, her tongue darting out to meet with his. Then she stopped and looked at him. 'I've wanted to do this all night.'

'Really?' The idea came as a shock at first, but then he shouldn't be surprised. If he were truthful, so had he. Everything about last night had felt so … right between them. As if this was meant to be.

'So have I,' he agreed, with a wolfish grin.

'I don't normally … well, you know … do this sort of thing with men on the first date.' The grin left her lips as her blue eyes became serious.

'What, sleep with them?'

'Oh.' Her mouth formed the perfect O of surprise and he had to laugh out loud. 'No, I would never …'

'It's okay,' he said, 'I'm just teasing. I don't normally … well, you know …' He was about to say he didn't normally do this sort of thing either.

'Ahoy in there,' a voice sounded from outside.

'Shit, they're here already.' Dusty wanted to yell and curse. They couldn't have timed it any worse. But instead he carefully maneuvered out from beneath Lana and stepped onto the cold wooden floor. 'Sorry,' he breathed as he pulled on his crumpled jeans and reached for his shirt. She just gave him a rueful smile as he threw her now dry sweater at her.

Dusty gave his own grim smile in return and reached to open the door. Four men in bright orange overalls stood outside on a carpet of white. Snow coated everything in a magical shroud.

'How's it going, Dusty?' The lead man extended his hand for Dusty to shake.

'Hi, Paddy.' Dusty took his hand. He recognized the local mechanic from the next town. 'She's here, come on in.'

'Thanks, Dusty, we'll take it from here.' He opened the door wider and let Paddy and one of the other men inside; their small sanctuary now forever shattered.

An hour later, Dusty and Scout made their slow way back down the mountain. The appaloosa was showing no ill effects from being cooped up in a wood shed all night. The horse had stopped for a long drink of icy water from the snow-fed stream at the bottom of the ridge. And he'd more than deserve that bin of feed waiting for him back in the stables when they finally got home. Come to think of it, Dusty could do with a good hot meal as well. He'd heated up another tin of baked beans for Lana this morning, but he hadn't eaten anything. He hadn't felt like food, for some reason.

The SES search team had arranged for the Westpac rescue helicopter to come and pick Lana up. There was a clearing a few hundred meters away. Not big enough to land in, but big enough so the helicopter could get low and winch her up without incident.

Once the SES team arrived, there hadn't been a chance to speak to Lana alone again. Dusty stood back and let them go about their business. But just as Paddy led her down the single step from the mountain hut, she turned and grabbed him by the arm. He searched her face, imprinting it on his memory, taking in her aquiline nose, the small nose ring beneath it, and her elfin features, still dwarfed by his stupid knit cap.

'I'll be back soon,' she said. 'And we need to talk. I want to talk to you.' Her sky-blue eyes had fixed on his, and right at that moment, he believed her. Believed that something passed between them, a spark, a pledge of some sort. She would be back. He wanted her to come back.

But now, as he and his horse wended their way through the drifts of snow, back towards his little farm, the words seemed to fade into the vaporous clouds above. Who was he kidding? He made a living here, on his small farm. Just making ends meet. It was hard work, but he wouldn't give it up for the world. She was a city girl. She wouldn't want what he could give her. He'd just imagined it. Nothing had passed between them. He'd rescued a city girl from freezing to death one day. That was all. There was nothing more to it.

Scout snorted, emitting a cloud of white steam in the cold morning air.

'I know, mate. I want to go home, too.' Patting the horse's neck, he urged him down the mountain. Better go and check how many sheep he'd lost in the storm.

Lana

Lana stared out her office window. Sydney was a blurry tumult of differently hued grays below. Low gloomy clouds draped over the city like a veil. The water in the harbor was the color of steel, whipped to white caps by the wind. The tall city buildings around her were only misty outlines in the all-encompassing drizzle. The day corresponded exactly to the way she was feeling. Grey and sad and miserable.

Hugging her arms even tighter around herself, she shivered. She couldn't seem to get warm. Even the beautiful pink Chanel vintage skirt and matching jacket constricted her chest, itched her neck and all she wanted to do was rip it off and put on her comfy tracksuit instead. Normally the view from her office, twenty stories up, inspired her. But not today. Carefully, she rested her forehead against the cold glass of the window.

She didn't want to be here. Couldn't be here.

'Hello, Ehlana. How are you feeling today?' She twitched guiltily and stood up straight. Getting her features under control, she turned around slowly.

'Fine thanks, Dad.'

'Yes, well you should be fine. It's been over a week now, since you returned. It's high time you threw yourself back into work. I'm glad to see you finally made it.'

'Mmm hmm.' She didn't trust herself to speak. There were all kinds of words hovering at the back of her throat she wanted to spit out at her father. But it was her first day back at work, the least she could do was try and be civil towards him.

The first day or so after her ordeal, when she'd returned from the hospital weak and pale, but physically fine after her night out in the cold, her father offered hesitant compassion. Had even come around to her flat to make sure she was really okay. Which was almost unheard of. Her father didn't approve of her small flat in Paddington, thought she should rent something more modern, more suitable to the job she was now doing. After all, he gave her everything she needed, bought her expensive clothes and a car. He was proud of the fact his architect company was now one of the biggest in Sydney, constantly reminded her how hard he'd had to work to attain his dream. And he liked her and Gail to look the part, just as he did in his designer suits and big mansion on the bay. Little did he know she'd chosen the flat not just because of its proximity to the arts scene, or because of its bohemian, grungy style, but also because she knew it would annoy him greatly.

But as the days dragged on and Lana still didn't show up for work, his phone calls became less understanding and more demanding. And really, he was probably right. There was no tangible reason why she shouldn't return to work. How could she tell him that it almost made her physically sick to think about walking through those big glass doors of the high-rise building and back to her job.

Even her sister, Gail, became increasingly worried about her.

'What really happened to you up there? Perhaps you hit your head and you don't remember?' she'd said the night before last, when she'd called in with takeaway Chinese food, to find Lana curled up on the couch in her pajamas. Gail lived on the University campus, said she loved the lifestyle. It was highly unusual for her to call in unannounced like this.

'I'm fine, the doctors cleared me of all that kind of thing,' Lana replied wearily.

'Then what's wrong with you?' Gail demanded. Her younger sister had sounded almost scared. 'Why are you acting so … I don't know, it's like you're depressed or something. But why would you be depressed?' Little did Gail know she'd actually hit the nail right on the head. In a way Lana was depressed. There was nothing physically wrong with her. It was all in her head.

Because she was missing Dusty. Missing the mountains.

That one night in the hut with Dusty held more meaning for her than the past six months spent working in her father's company. As if she'd been floating along in a dream, only half-living. And then Dusty had awoken something inside her. A flame. A flame that if she allowed it to flare was going to change her whole life.

She'd spoken to Dusty just the once since she returned home. He'd called her on the second day home from hospital, though Lana had no idea how he got her number. Perhaps she had Aunt Joyce to thank for that. Just checking she really was oaky after her ordeal. It'd been so nice to hear his voice, unwanted tears sprang to her eyes. Which was stupid, she wasn't the sentimental type, certainly not when it came to man she'd known for less than two days.

Once she found her voice and once she convinced him she was physically fine, they'd talked for over an hour. Like old friends, about silly mundane things, like how he had names for all the alpacas on his farm and how she secretly loved to watch the show Survivor on TV. After she hung up the phone, Lana sat in her empty flat and ached to jump in her car and drive right back up to the mountains.

'I'm fine,' she'd told Gail. 'I'm just thinking. There are some decisions I need to make.' Lana hadn't told her father much about her rescue, just the bare facts, which he'd taken at face value and quickly moved on. She'd mentioned to Gail about spending the night in a hut to weather the blizzard but hadn't hinted anything about what had truly gone on between herself and Dusty.

Only Aunt Joyce and Uncle Tom knew the details. That Dusty helped keep her warm by wrapping them both up in the blankets together. But even they didn't know how much Dusty affected Lana. How he'd touched her heart in that short space of time. More than any other man had ever done.

Lana's last relationship ended nearly a year ago. During her final exams for her uni degree. Brian said she was selfish, spending too much time studying and not enough time with him. He wanted someone who'd concentrate on his needs more. Which was fair enough, if that's what he wanted. The breakup was surprisingly unexceptional, a bit like the whole relationship really. And she'd gone on to ace her exams.

There were other men before Dusty, but now it was almost as if she couldn't remember a single one of them. Dusty was the one burned into her brain. She hardly knew him, but she wanted to get to know him. Oh so badly.

It wasn't just Dusty himself affecting her. It was the idea he'd planted in her head. The seed of possibility. The idea of taking what she wanted, the dream, and turning it into reality.

'Lana.' Her father's sharp reprimand brought her focus back from the past. She needed to have a conversation with him. And now was as good as time as any. 'Have you got the Stanley file ready for me to go over? It's an important job, I want to make sure you haven't missed anything.'

Taking a deep breath, Lana squared her shoulders and took a step forward.

'Dad, I need to talk to you.' He wasn't going to like what she had to say, but suddenly, just saying those words made her feel lighter, as if a weight had lifted from her shoulders. She was making the right decision, she just knew it.

Dusty

Dusty stared morosely at Bombur. The alpaca stared right back at him with deep intelligent eyes. Bombur was a rich chocolate color and Dusty secretly thought of him as his favorite. The alpaca's head butted gently against Dusty's chest to get his attention, hoping he might have a treat hidden in one of his pockets somewhere.

His mother thought the farm would be more sustainable if they branched out a little, didn't put all their eggs in one basket. The alpacas were her idea, her babies really. She wanted to breed them for their fleece, which was a rapidly growing industry in Australia. He'd agreed with her, mainly because his pastures were pretty good and alpacas didn't require too much in feed supplements or other costly additions. And they were definitely smarter than sheep. And cuter.

The summer before his mother got sick, they'd shorn the alpacas for the first time and Dusty had been more than surprised at the profit they made from the sale of the fleeces. In the two years since his mum died, Dusty had kept the herd ticking over, but hadn't really paid as much attention as he perhaps should have. The potential to make more money from the alpacas than he was making from the sheep was there, it just had to be built up properly.

Bombur butted him again with his shaggy head and gave a low humming bleat making Dusty laugh.

'Silly old thing,' he said to the persistent animal.

Lana had laughed when he told her he'd named all the alpacas after the dwarves in The Lord of the Rings. Bombur was named because normally he was the fattest animal in the herd. But he was looking decidedly thin recently, losing condition and Dusty didn't know why.

Parasites probably. He kept the herd well drenched for worms, but perhaps there was something he was missing. Dusty would need to make a call to Bruce, the local vet to get a proper diagnosis. Another bill he didn't need right now. But he couldn't get rid of the alpacas. They'd belonged to his mother.

He leaned up against the top wooden rail of the holding yard, Bombur standing companionably by his side. Scout ambled up from the other side of the fence and blew warm air into Dusty's nose.

'Hiya, boy.' At least Scout was still healthy and strong. And hungry. He needed to go and break open another bale of hay for the horse. Snow still lay on the ground, turning the yards into a muddy obstacle course. The wind tried to pierce through the opening of his coat and he zipped it right up to his chin to keep the cold out.

The coat Lana had worn when he rescued her.

He wished he could hear her laugh again.

That laugh which'd sounded down the phone line the other day when he rang her to make sure she was all recovered. But now he had no more reasons to call her. No more reasons to hear her voice again.

It'd been as if they were old friends when they talked on the phone. When it came time to say goodbye, he'd wanted to ask her out, on a date. Had to force the words back down his throat. Because it was just a fantasy. She lived in the city. He lived here, far away, in the country. There was no way their lives could ever intersect. It'd been nearly three weeks now, since he rescued Lana. Three long weeks, where images of her petite face and blue eyes would come to him at the oddest of moments. While he was standing in the kitchen, waiting for the microwave to finish heating his frozen dinner. While he was stacking the logs of wood he'd just chopped into a neat pile next to the back door. While he was lying in bed, desperately trying to get to sleep.

Lana had opened doors he forgotten were even closed. Opened up his heart to possibilities. Shown him the truth.

He was lonely, living out here on his own, with only the alpacas and sheep for company.

Since Mum died there was just so much to do around the place, he never stopped long enough to let it get to him. Or at least that's what he'd been telling himself. But now he knew it wasn't true. A girl with a nose ring had proven that.

Perhaps it was time to do something about it. Stop living like a hermit. Maybe he should start going into town more often. Attending the local community events, like the weekly markets or go to the pub for a social beer every now and then. A few of the single local women had tried to tempt him over the past years. He'd even started seeing Lindy, who worked at the local bank a few months before his mum got sick. Things were going well, he even spent the occasional night at her house. But things had come to a grinding halt when his mum was diagnosed. She wanted to keep seeing him, but he said it wasn't fair, he was just too engrossed with caring for his mother. And after Mum died, well he just hadn't the strength to even try anymore.

There was a trivia night planned for next Saturday at the community hall. He was bad at trivia, but that wasn't really the point. Sally Harman had invited him last week, while he'd been standing in line at the gas station, waiting to pay.

Sally was a widower, her husband killed in a car accident a few years ago. She was brash and loud, large breasts out for all to see and not at all what Dusty was looking for in a woman. But he had to admire her, at least she was still living life. Not letting herself moulder away in some dilapidated farmhouse, alone and lonely. At least she had the courage and strength to keep looking for love. Even if she was barking up the wrong tree when it came to him.

Perhaps he would join Sally's table at the trivia night after all. As long as she understood it was purely friends, nothing more. Get himself out there again.

Open himself up to the possibilities of love once more.

If only it were Lana who he was going to the trivia night with.

With a big sigh, he swiveled on his heel and made his way out through the gate, leaving an unimpressed bleating alpaca behind him.

Time to go an ring the vet. And time to light the fire and get inside, before the night descended and froze him to the spot.

Toeing his mud-caked boots off at the back door, he was just in time to hear the phone ring.

Who was calling at this time of evening? His phone hardly ever rang. Probably some marketing company trying to sell him something. He hated those cold-callers. The pile of wood in his arms was dropped with a thud next to the fireplace as he stomped over to the table in the living room that held the landline.

'Hello' His tone was gruff, but he didn't care. He was hungry and cold and wanted whoever it was on the phone to be gone.

'Dusty? Is that you?' The voice on the other end was hesitant, as if she wasn't sure she'd rung the right number.

'Lana?' His heart rate skyrocketed.

Lana

'Hi, Dusty.' Lana couldn't keep the tremble out of her voice. Goddamnit, why was she so nervous? 'I'm glad you could make it.' He stood next to his old Toyota ute in her uncle's driveway, awkward and unsure. Broad shoulders hunched uncertainly, he managed to give her a quick smile.

'Hiya.' His voice was still as gruff and deep as she remembered. 'Well, your invitation was a little cryptic. How could I resist?' He looked as good as she remembered, too. No, better. Tall and straight, he stood gazing down at her, brown eyes sparkling. She wanted to knock that dirty old Akubra hat right off his head and run her hands through that wonderful thick black hair. A bit of decorum was called for, however, and she managed to contain herself. Her aunt and uncle were here, watching. But it was hard. She was about to burst with a mixture of excitement and trepidation and joy, all rolled into one.

'It's so good to see you again.' She couldn't help herself then, she had to throw her arms around his neck and hug him. And it was just as she'd imagined it would be. A month of hoping this moment would happen hadn't dulled the reality one single bit. He felt solid and real beneath her hands. Ridding her of the last vestiges of doubt. She hadn't dreamt her time in the hut with him after all. Hadn't dreamt how she felt about him. His arms came up around her, holding her tight against his body.

'Good to see you, too.' His reply was a little muffled because her arms were still around her neck. The heels of her boots landed back on the gravel, and she finally let him go.

'And good to see you properly attired this time,' he added with a nod towards her feather-down coat. Even though the snow was just about gone, with spring on the horizon, it was still a dull, cold day, with heavy clouds promising rain. As if to highlight that thought, the dull grumble of thunder echoed off the surrounding hills.

'Yes, I learned my lesson. I never leave the house now without a good coat on.' She smiled in response. It was true, never again would she underestimate the power of Mother Nature. She stared at him, caught in the depths of his eyes, until he shifted uncomfortably.

'How have you been? How's the farm?' It was a mundane question, but she knew the farm was important to Dusty. Tom had filled her in on the details, after she'd asked him to make some discreet inquiries around town, while she was still down in Sydney, recovering. Lana knew Dusty left some of his sheep out in the storm when he'd come to rescue her. She hated to think she might've been a source of misery and financial loss to him. But the news had been good. Dusty only lost two sheep that night. Somehow they'd managed to find shelter under a stand of snow gums, away from the worst of the snowfall.

'Good. It's all going good.'

'That's great,' she replied chirpily. But she could see the unasked question hovering in his eyes. Time to get on with the reason she'd asked him here today. 'I wanted you to be the first to see it.' Now it was her turn to be shy and awkward. What if he hated it? Bracing her shoulders, she straightened her back. If she wanted to be a proper painter, then she needed to get over all these self-doubts. But after so many years, the habit was hard to break. 'I think you've already met Joyce and Tom.' Belatedly, she introduced her uncle and aunt.

'Tom, how's it going?' Dusty extended his hand in greeting. 'Joyce, good to see you again, too.' But Joyce dispensed with the pleasantries and followed Lana's lead, taking Dusty in a big, bear hug. Lana winced. It wouldn't do to scare the man away before she'd even had a chance to show him what she was planning.

'Come this way,' she said and grabbed his hand, rescuing him from Joyce's clutches. They walked towards the large work shed at the end of driveway, Tom and Joyce trailing behind.

'What am I looking at?'

'Well …' She wasn't sure how to voice her hopes and dreams and aspirations, so instead she flung open the double doors to the shed and led him inside.

'It's an art exhibition.' And there in front of them, filling every available space, were all her paintings, arranged in neat, symmetrical rows, on easels, hanging from wires, attached to every wall of the shed. It did look good, she had to admit. Tom and Joyce had helped her over the past week. They'd moved all the old equipment and boxes and tools and other paraphernalia out and into a corner of the wool shed at the back of the property, so there was room for her paintings.

Her aunt and uncle had become accomplices in her dream. They'd been the ones to plant the seed in the first place after all, and they were only too happy to help her out now. The second she'd rung her uncle with the idea, he'd said yes immediately, without even waiting for her to finish outlining the plan.

'You know we love you like a daughter,' Tom had said. 'Of course you can move in with us.' She couldn't help it, she'd cried, standing in the kitchen of her small flat, on the other end of the phone. She'd cried because her dream might actually come true. And she'd cried because her aunt and uncle believed in her. When her own father wouldn't.

'Wow! Oh, wow.' Dusty's eyes went as wide as saucers. 'These are amazing.' He trailed slowly down the first row of paintings, looking at each one. 'You are amazing.' He stopped and stared at her. 'You should definitely sell these.'

'Thank you.' She was genuinely humbled by his reaction. It was a reaction she'd been hoping for, but never truly believed would happen. Until now. Her heart swelled as she contemplated Dusty. The look of awe grew on his face as he kept moving and she walked slowly after him. Tom and Joyce stood in the doorway and watched. 'Actually, you're a bit of a guinea pig for this whole thing.'

'What?' Confusion replaced the awe on his features.

'Well, Joyce has helped me organize an exhibition in a small local gallery.' She glanced quickly at her aunt, who gave her an encouraging nod. 'Her friend runs it, and they just happened to have an opening where I can showcase my collection next month. And I have a professional photographer coming to take photos tomorrow. To send to a big dealer in Sydney, who's interested in displaying some of my paintings in their gallery.'

'That's great news, Lana.'

'I know. But if you hated it, then I was going to cancel it all.'

'You're kidding. Why?' There was shock in his deep voice.

'Because I trust your judgment. And because it's a really big, scary step for me.'

'I'm not sure I'm the best person to ask,' Dusty said with a grimace and looked towards Joyce and Tom for assistance. They nodded at him encouragingly. 'But if you want my opinion, then you should go for it. These paintings are the best thing I've seen in a long time. They deserve to be put in the spotlight, so other people can see how talented you are.'

'Really? You really think so?'

'Yes. I know so.' The shine in his eyes told her everything he was trying to convey in those few words. But she had more to tell him. And she hoped he liked this news just as much.

'Also, I've moved out here temporarily. I'm going to live with Tom and Joyce for six months. I've taken leave without pay, to see how it goes.' And hadn't her father just loved that news. But she'd weathered the storm and stuck to her guns.

Just then another rumble of thunder sounded, closer now. The clouds looked even lower when she peeked out through the shed door. That's when she noticed her aunt and uncle were no longer there. Had sneaked off to go back inside, probably to put the kettle on, and left them in peace to talk. She was so grateful to them, so glad she'd taken the chance. The chance to fulfill her ambition.

Another rumble of thunder reverberated through the corrugated iron roof, sounding like it was almost directly overhead. Then a flash of lightening lit up the doorway.

'Wow, did you see that. Come on.' She grabbed his hand and towed him back outside. There was nothing better than watching a lightening show as it made a spectacle over the mountains in the distance. She led him down the side of the shed, towards the back fence, where they could see Mt Jagungal in the distance.

'I'm glad I'm not out there tonight,' she whispered still holding his hand. A few wet splashes hit her, and she turned her face up to receive the rain.

'So am I,' Dusty replied. 'I'm so glad I listened to my gut instinct that day. So glad it was me who found you. I never told you this, but it was almost as if someone, or something was telling me to go and find you.'

Wow, she never thought to hear those kinds of words come from Dusty's lips. But then again, she was glad she'd followed her gut, too.

'So, you know, now I'm going to be living here. If you're free for dinner one night, I'm a pretty good cook.' Her heart was beating wildly in her chest, but she kept her face turned up to the sky, pretending to watch the lightening, afraid to look him in the eye. What would he say?

'Are you asking me on a date?' He stepped in closer. So close she could feel his breath pulse past her cheek.

'I guess I am.' She wanted to giggle, but when he closed the gap between them until there was nowhere for her to go, her heart pounded in her chest and chased away any vestige of humor. The rain started to come down much harder now, leaving droplets in his hair, turning his shoulders damp.

'Then my answer is yes.' His strong arms came up and gathered her into his chest. Oh God, that same feeling came flooding back. The one when she'd laid in his arms in the hut. A buzzing need, a rightness, a sincerity. Her blood turned molten in her veins. Then he leaned in and kissed her. His lips gentle yet demanding. She hardly headed the rain, as it got harder and more insistent. They would soon be soaked through. But she wasn't the slightest bit cold. She was warm and safe in Dusty's arms. All other thoughts fled. It was just her and Dusty. Kissing in the rain. Together. At last.

LOST AND FOUND

Suzanne Cass

Kita

'I'll get there as quick as I can. See you soon, Blake.' Kita hit the End button and stared thoughtfully at her phone. Then she looked down beside her chair, to where a pair of intelligent brown eyes watched her every move.

'Time to go to work, Leroy.' The dog's ears pricked forward at her words and his tail thumped loudly on the wooden floor. 'There's a girl lost up on Mt Jagungal, and they need your nose. What do you think, are we up to the task?'

The dog stood up, his feathery tail working double time. Whatever was going on, he wanted to be involved. Leroy was a Border Collie cross, or so the woman at the dog shelter told her when she chose him from the row of wiggling pups, all desperate for love and attention. Highly intelligent the woman had said. Too intelligent for his own good, Kita sometimes thought. Which is why she'd started training with the State Emergency Services volunteer search and rescue group, or SES. To give Leroy an outlet for his clever doggy brain.

A cold chill snaked down Kita's spine. This was her and Leroy's first real call-out. Were they up to the task? They'd spent enough time training for the real thing, out working as a team nearly every weekend for the past eighteen months. Leroy was certified as an operational dog two months ago.

He had the coveted tag on his dog jacket now proclaiming his name, along with her name as his handler, below it. Blake, the team leader, was quietly confident in them.

'Come on. Let's do this.' Kita stood up and Leroy immediately began to dance his enthusiastic doggy dance around her, toenails clicking on the wooden floor. At least one of them was excited. When he saw she was heading towards the back door, where she kept his lead, his dance became so enthusiastic he nearly knocked her feet from under her.

'Settle down,' she growled, but her tone was only mildly disapproving. She was too nervous to get mad at him. She needed this to go well. *They* needed this to go well.

There was a pile of neatly folded thick woolen sweaters on top of the dryer. She grabbed the first one and pulled it over her head. Then her hand stalled halfway up to the peg that held Leroy's lead. Bugger. She remembered her car was in the auto repair shop. Bugger, bugger, bugger. It might be fixed by now, the guy hadn't been sure how long it'd take when she'd dropped it in yesterday. It'd started making some kind of awful clunking noise on the way home from visiting her friend Rachael, and it was just lucky she'd been passing the mechanic shop. It really was time she bought herself a new car. It wasn't like she couldn't afford it. The car had belonged to Will, and up till now she couldn't bring herself to sell it. The man at the auto shop hadn't been sure what was wrong, but promised to call her as soon as he had some news. That'd been almost twenty-four hours ago. Surely it must be fixed by now.

She needed that car. She couldn't let Blake down now, not on their first proper call-out. And not with a girl missing in the mountains. With a possible blizzard predicted soon. Not good conditions for anyone to be out in the wilderness. Especially not someone who was ill-prepared.

Shrugging into her special-issue SES weatherproof coat,

she went back into the living room and threw a few more large logs into the old cast-iron wood-burning stove. They'd burn for the next six to eight hours if she damped the stove right down, and keep her small cottage warm for when she finally returned home.

The auto shop wasn't too far away, she would walk over and see if her car was ready. The backpack she kept ready for just such a call sat waiting in the hallway. There was a bottle of water, some high-protein snacks, gloves, a knit-cap, spare socks and basic first aid equipment. The SES bright orange coveralls sat neatly folded next to the pile of sweaters. She pushed them into the backpack, ready to change into once she got to the site, along with Leroy's orange working jacket proclaiming him as a rescue dog. Once that jacket went on his back, he knew it meant time to work. Slinging the backpack over her shoulder, there was no need to whistle up Leroy, because he was bouncing at her feet, giving impatient little whines because she was taking so long.

Locking her door, Kita trudged up the steep driveway and into the street. Force of habit had her turning around so she could take in the view over Lake Jindabyne. A bitter wind marauded around the trees lining the foreshore, finding its way into the tiny gaps in her coat. The man-made lake was deep and wide, with small whitecaps floating on top of the steel grey water. Low clouds hung over the surrounding hill tops, which were dotted with the odd eucalyptus tree. Will had loved this place. But right now she was finding it hard to understand why. This small alpine town survived on tourists, skiers in the winter and hikers in the summer. But that was about all it had to offer as far as Kita was concerned. She should just move back to Perth. At least that's what her mum kept telling her. Then she could be with her family. What was the point of staying in this town? Now that Will was gone.

At least her self-made business, where she helped other

small businesses develop their own solid marketing platforms, kept her financially viable. She could do everything on her laptop from home. Thank God for the internet. So, she could live anywhere she chose.

An image of her mum's displeased face hovered in her mind. Her mum was Japanese, small and slight—much like Kita—and very prim and proper. A stickler for the rules. But even her prim and proper mother had a streak of rebellion, and it'd come out when she'd fallen in love with Kita's father. The epitome of an English gentleman, tall blonde and dapper. Kita smiled at the memory. They made such a sweet couple, still in love, even after all these years. She had her mother's dark hair and almond-shaped eyes. Will had always said her Eurasian ancestry made her completely stunning, but she'd always laughed and called him silly.

'Hmph,' Kita said as she pulled the zipper on her coat right up to her chin. As usual, she pushed the memories of Will and her family to the back of her mind. For some reason she wasn't ready to leave Jindabyne yet. Even though there was nothing left for her here.

'Come on, boofhead,' she said to Leroy and he bounced eagerly up the road, towing her behind him.

Ten minutes later, Kita walked across a large concrete carpark toward a huddle of brick buildings with a large warehouse squatting next to them. The place looked deserted. The big roller door which normally opened up onto the auto shop floor was closed. Not a good sign. But she could hear banging coming from inside, so she took a deep breath and walked towards a door in the side. The handle turned beneath her fingers and she peered through the crack in the doorway. The pungent smell of grease hit her first, and it took a while for her eyes to adjust to the gloom inside. The place was lit by a bank of fluorescent lights. Leroy lifted his nose and tested the air.

'Hello? Is anyone in here?'

The banging stopped, but no one answered.

She called out again, a little louder this time, 'Hello.'

Three cars were parked in a row, taking up most of the space in the warehouse. The middle one was hers. A large metal bench ran the whole length of the far wall, covered in all kinds of tools and engine parts, dirty rags and bottles of oil. It looked like any typical auto shop might.

'Hello?' A deep male voice echoed around the shop. Then a head popped up from behind the last car in the row. The man gave her a quizzical look which wasn't entirely friendly. Obviously, he didn't like being disturbed.

'Sorry, luv, we're closed,' he said as he got to his feet and dusted off his grey coveralls. Although, they were already so covered in grease stains and dirt Kita wondered why he bothered.

'I'm sorry, I thought you were open till five,' she replied, trying to keep the defensiveness out of her tone. And the desperation.

'Not on Saturday, luv. We close at twelve on Saturday.' The man gave her a grin that seemed to say it was the end of the conversation. But she wasn't giving up that quickly.

'That's my car over there. The white Audi. I was just wondering if it's ready to go yet?'

He shook his head in a resigned fashion and wended his way between the cars towards her. Now she could see him properly in the light, she took in his longish blonde hair, pulled back into a man-bun, and his strong jawline, covered in a three-day scruff. There was a smudge of grease under his left eye. And as he finally came to stand in front of her, she could see those eyes were a cobalt blue. Bright and intelligent, but evidently not happy at the interruption.

'Sorry, your car won't be ready till the middle of next week. Marco was supposed to call and let you know.' The man frowned as if silently berating whoever this Marco fellow was. Then his frown turned into a smile as Leroy, tired of waiting for an introduction, stuck his nose against the man's hand and gave it a lick.

'Hey, boy.' He patted Leroy's head and Leroy gave the man his best doggy smile in return, tail beating the air.

'I really need my car,' Kita said. 'I need to get somewhere, fast. Can I take it now and bring it back later to be fixed?'

'Sorry, luv, the car's in bits.'

Her irritation rose as he called her luv again, but as she walked around to the front of her car, she could see what he meant. Her car was undrivable, the whole front end had been taken apart. Her heart sank.

'We're waiting for a part to come in. You had a really worn tie rod.' At her look of incomprehension, he added, 'That's the part that connects your steering wheel to the steering arm. It's effectively how you steer the car. If that breaks suddenly, you'll end up in a ditch, or worse.'

'Oh no.' Now what was she going to do? Blake had asked her to get out to the Mt Jagungal carpark near the town of Dandang as soon as she could. All the volunteers would meet there, have a briefing and be out searching as soon as possible. She was tempted to go up and kick the car, but restrained herself, knowing it'd make her look crazier than she already did.

'Sorry,' the man said again. 'Marco was supposed to call you, I'm gonna have a few things to say to him on Monday. You're lucky I was even here. I was just about to head home myself.'

She stared at him, not sure what to say or do. She needed a car. She couldn't let Blake down now. Or herself. The man stared back, slight confusion clouding his nice blue eyes. Randomly, she noticed he was rather good-looking. Could perhaps even pass as a brother to Chris Hemsworth.

Where had that thought come from? She needed to focus.

'Oh. Right.' Kita tried to get her thoughts back under control. 'I don't suppose you have a loan car you could give me for the day?'

He shook his head, but the look of confusion on his face was turning to one of concern.

'Look, my name's James, I own the business. But I'm really sorry, we don't have a loan car. Do you mind if I ask what the big hurry is all about? Is there some kind of emergency?'

James

Why couldn't he keep his mouth shut? James watched the woman as her hand fluttered up to her mouth. She was worried about something, that much was obvious. Bloody hell. The absolute last thing he needed was a fraught woman on his doorstep. All he wanted was to go home, have a shower, grab a beer or two and sink into the oblivion of watching some mind-numbing TV. It was Saturday afternoon, he needed a break.

The woman's gaze flittered helplessly around his shop and he found himself repeating his last words, much to his internal exasperation. 'Is there something I can help you with? Some kind of emergency?'

'No. I mean … yes, there is a sort of emergency.' Her gaze stopped flickering around the warehouse and finally came to rest on him. Her eyes were dark brown, a nice almond shape, with long dark lashes. Olive skin and long black hair, pulled into a ponytail that fell almost to her waist. A hint that perhaps one of her parents was of Asian descent.

His eyes dropped to the dog, sitting patiently at her feet. Cute dog, and well-behaved. Some sort of Border Collie cross if he wasn't mistaken. Mostly black, the dog had white front paws, a white blaze on his chest and gray ears and muzzle. A sudden ache pulsed in his chest. An ache of loss for his own dog, Gem. God how he missed that cheeky lopsided grin the dog used to get whenever he'd greet him at the door after a long day at work. That bitch ex-wife had stolen Gem from him. Just like she'd stolen everything else.

'A girl is missing, up on Mt Jagungal.'

James shook his head. 'What?' He wasn't following how that affected this lady and her dog.

'We're part of the SES canine unit. They need us up there as soon as possible.' A frown furrowed her pretty brow.

'Oh.' It was making a horrible kind of sense now. The orange and black coat she was wearing finally registered in his brain as the one the search and rescue volunteers normally wore. She needed her car to get out to the search site. And it was in pieces, not going anywhere for at least a few days. But this could be fixed, couldn't it? There must be a solution, she just hadn't thought about it properly.

'Is there someone you can call to give you a lift?' Didn't this woman have any friends who could help her?

'No, everyone else has already gone.' She bit her bottom lip with her top teeth, worry causing tiny wrinkles at the corners of her almond-shaped eyes. 'I'd normally ask Rachael, but she's down in Cooma this weekend. There's no one else,' she repeated. 'Are you sure you couldn't loan me a car? Anything?'

Jesus, why did he always get stuck with the needy women? He wanted to tell her to go and bother someone else. That she wasn't his problem. But in a way she was. Because her car was sitting in pieces in his workshop and his mechanic hadn't bothered to tell her she'd be without a car this weekend. Bloody hell. He ran a hand over his hair, feeling the tufts that'd escaped the elastic.

'Fine, give me a few minutes to close up here. I'll drive you out there.' He couldn't believe he was uttering these words. His shower and beer would have to wait.

'What?' Her expression said she wasn't completely happy with his solution. And to be fair, she didn't know him at all, so she was right to be wary of jumping in a car with a strange man.

'Look, lady, it's the only solution I can see to your problem. Take it or leave it.'

She hesitated, staring up at him. She was petite, perhaps only just five foot, almost child-like in her bulky coat.

'Um … I don't know.' She looked around quickly, reminding him of a rabbit caught in a snare. 'Okay. Leroy seems to think you're alright, so I'll trust you too. Yes, I'll let you take me out to the mountain.'

Let him take her? The woman had some kind of nerve. He was doing her a favor, not the other way around.

'I need to go home and change first. I'll only be five minutes,' he added when her eyes widened in concern. 'I'm not going out there like this. I'm dirty and I'll freeze to death without a proper coat.'

'Oh, okay, thanks. My name's Kita, by the way, and this is Leroy.'

'Nice to meet you,' he muttered. 'My car is the white Land Cruiser ute out the front. You can go and tie your dog in the back and I'll meet you out there soon. I'll just shut up in here.'

'Thanks.' She still seemed unsure, but he wasn't about to mollycoddle her. She either wanted a lift or she didn't.

Five minutes later he pulled into his driveway and shut off the engine.

'Nice house,' she said.

He snorted. It might well have been a nice house once, but now it was hard to see it through the tall weeds staking out the front yard. He should do something about them. Normally, it didn't bother him, but following Kita's gaze he could suddenly see it from her perspective. And it wasn't pretty. But then he'd let lots of things go, after Bridget left him.

The house was built into the side of a hill, double story, with a great view back over the lake. He and Bridget designed every last detail inside the large, colonial-style house. It'd cost him everything he had and more to buy his half back off her when she left. And sometimes he wondered why he'd even bothered. On those odd occasions when he actually thought clearly about the divorce, he freely admitted it was more to spite her than for any real longing to keep the house for himself.

'Do you want to come in? I need to get changed and grab a few things, but I won't be long.'

To his surprise she nodded, and hopped out, then reached into the back to untie her dog. He led her up the steps onto the first-floor verandah.

'After you.' He held the door open for her to precede him.

'Wow, it's gorgeous,' she said, tipping her head back to take in the high vaulted ceilings. 'And your kitchen is to die for.' She walked into the open-plan kitchen, running a hand over the gray marble bench top.

Her fingers were fine-boned and delicate. He liked the way they rested gently on the surface, as if reading the story left behind in the polished finish.

'I bet you make some wonderful meals in here,' she said with a hint of envy.

'Yep,' he grunted. If only she knew. This kitchen hadn't been used properly for a long time. Not that he wasn't a good cook, because when the mood took him, he was. It was just easier to heat up a meal in the microwave when you were only catering for one. Food was a fuel to keep the body going. It was usually the beverages that accompanied the meal he was more interested in.

'Can I let Leroy out in your back yard for a second? He needs a wee break.'

'What? Oh, sure.' Her subject change caught him by surprise. 'The back door is through the kitchen, over that way.' He pointed. 'I'll just go and change my clothes and make a thermos of coffee to go.' They'd need something to keep them warm if they were going up into the mountains on a day like today. Flicking on the kettle, he made his way upstairs to his bedroom, already undoing the buttons on his coveralls. They could do with a clean, he couldn't remember the last time he washed them. And he also couldn't remember the last time he'd cared, either. Strange.

On his way back down the stairs a few minutes later, he jumped when a voice caught him unawares. Shit, he thought she was still outside.

'Those sculptures are amazing. Did you make them?'

'Oh, um, yeah. I used to. Haven't done anything for a while.' Bugger, he'd forgotten they were out there. Showed how long it'd been since he'd ventured out in the back yard.

'That's a shame. The one of the snake, or was it a python? Made out of chains. It scared me half to death. I thought it was real for a second.' She gave a girlish laugh. A tinkling sound that made the hair on his forearms stand up. How long since a woman had laughed in this house?

Kita and Leroy waited for him at the bottom of the stairs, Leroy sitting obediently at her feet.

'And that one of the horse, right up the back near the fence. Wow. It was …' She seemed lost for words.

'It's just a bit of a hobby I used to do.' He waved a hand in the air dismissively. 'I used all the leftover scrap metal from the car parts and such. I should probably get rid of them all.' That was the truth. He was never going to do anything with those sculptures. Like he said, they were only a hobby. Perhaps he'd dreamed once that if they were good enough, people might actually buy them. But that was before. Now he lived in reality.

'I've boiled the kettle. I'll just fill the thermos and then we should get going,' he said, bustling around the kitchen.

The smile faded from her face. 'Yes, we should.'

Kita

The drive to Dandang took around an hour and Kita itched for James to drive faster. She needed to get there soon. Blake said he'd wait for her before they started the briefing. They needed her and Leroy, she was one of only two operational dogs in the area, and they'd be crucial in this search. But James was right to stick to the speed limit, especially on these tricky mountain roads. Thick eucalyptus forest sped past her window as she stared out at the road. Low clouds loomed, threatening rain—or worse, snow—soon. At least the car was warm and dry. She should make the most of it, she'd probably spend the rest of the afternoon getting cold, wet and hungry.

What should she say to this man beside her? This stranger. He wasn't much of a conversationalist. They'd sat in silence for the last ten minutes, as he drove them through the back streets of town and out onto the Alpine Way that would take them through the pass and onto the other side of the Snowy Mountain Range. Granted, he was gallant enough to offer to drive her out to the search site. So, she did owe him something.

'Thanks again for taking me,' she said. She'd probably ruined his afternoon off. What would a man like him do on a Saturday afternoon? For some reason she got the impression he wasn't married. His house didn't have that womanly touch to it. In fact, it'd seemed almost derelict and sterile, unloved. Which was a shame, because it really was a beautiful house.

And he wasn't wearing a ring.

Not that she was checking or anything, but his hand was resting on the steering wheel, right there for her to see.

Big, competent hands.

'It's the least I can do. The SES do a great job, and I know you're all volunteers. So I'm happy to help out.'

She cast a quick glance at him as he spoke. He'd changed into a woolen turtleneck sweater, chinos and heavy walking boots. The dark blue sweater set off his indigo eyes. Take away the greasy coveralls and James was even more handsome than when she'd first seen him back at the auto shop.

He looked nothing at all like Will.

Where had that thought come from?

'We need to turn onto Olsen's road. There's a carpark a few miles along, where we're all supposed to meet. Do you know it?'

'Yeah, I'll find it.' He took his eyes off the road briefly to give her a reassuring smile. 'I don't know a lot about the SES, but I didn't realize Jindabyne's little Snowy River Unit had a dog search crew.'

'It's relatively new. Blake Sampson was part of a dog unit down in Sydney and he moved up here a couple of years ago. Started recruiting potential dogs and their owners.'

'Nice. I probably should pay more attention to the SES, I've sometimes thought about joining up.'

'You should,' she agreed. 'They can always do with more volunteers.' They slipped into an easy conversation about the virtues of belonging to the volunteer society. Time passed quickly as she gazed at his handsome face and chatted. She even found herself telling him Leroy was the first dog, beside Blake's, to graduate and become operational, which was a much-needed boost to the little team.

Before she knew it, they were turning onto Olsen's Road. Her heart rate skipped up a few notches. Time to get to work.

The small carpark was overflowing with cars, mostly four-wheel drives, as well as people milling around. Some stood in small groups, talking, others hovered over piles of equipment. A large square tent with three sides had been set up in one corner. The crowd was thickest there, people flocking around the opening, their orange uniforms bright against the dark forest trees.

'Thanks,' Kita muttered, already opening the door, her focus moving away from the man in the car beside her as she watched the team mobilizing for the search. It wasn't the first time she'd seen this frantic gathering and speedy organization, she'd helped on a few searches as foot patrol in the past year. But this was the first time she'd be an integral part of the search. She and Leroy would play a pivotal role, along with Blake and his dog, Rusty. There were two other dog teams in training, but they were a long way from becoming operational.

The cold air hit her as she exited the car, her breath coming out in wispy tendrils. Much to Leroy's disgust, instead of untying him, she reached into the back of the ute and grabbed her backpack. He whined his protest, dark brown eyes never leaving her face. She proceeded to pull out her orange coveralls and drag them on over the top of her clothes. Then the black and orange weatherproof coat went back on over the top to complete the outfit. Once she was fully dressed, she stood on tiptoe to untie Leroy. He leapt out of the ute's tray like a gazelle, desperate to get going.

'Sit,' she commanded. He sat, eager tail thumping the ground. It was his turn to don his working gear, and she carefully strapped his orange jacket around his middle. Now they were both ready.

'Thanks again,' she said to James, who was leaning on the corner of the ute, watching. 'I'll be fine to get home from here, someone will give me a lift back down.'

'If you don't mind, I'll stay for a while.'

'Okay.' She shrugged. That was a surprise, she'd been sure he'd shoot off home as soon as his errand was complete. 'They'll be giving the briefing soon. You can follow me if you like.'

Her mind was only half on the man trailing behind her as she made her way toward the blue tent. She searched the crowd for anyone she knew. Damo might be here. He and his dog, Parker, a German Shepherd, were another trainee team, like herself. Trainee's weren't allowed to bring their dogs to real-life searches, but Damo should still be here, for moral support if nothing else. But there was no sign of him. The other dog team, a young woman called Sasha and her kelpie, Jaxon had only just started training with Blake a month or so ago, and they were often less than reliable. Sasha's heart was in the right place, she wanted to help, to become a part of the canine unit, but she was young and had a healthy social life. Kita couldn't see her amongst the crowd either.

Blake caught her eye over the top of the crowd. He was tall, over six foot four, distinguished and well-dressed, his sandy hair tinged gray around the temples. In some unfathomable way, Blake reminded her of her own father, always the English gentleman.

'Great, you made it,' Blake boomed over the chatter of the crowd.

Immediately everyone quieted down, and a few people turned in her direction. Was it just her imagination, or was that mild disapproval on some of their faces? They'd all been waiting for her to arrive.

'Come over here, Kita, near me, and we'll get this briefing under way.' Blake shooed a couple of people away from the front of the table to make a pathway for her. Without turning around, she could feel James following in her wake. Leroy bounded forwards to greet Rusty under the table.

'Who's this then?' Blake asked, holding out his hand at the same time.

'He gave me a lift out. Sorry, my car's broken down.'

'Glad you could come. Another warm body to lend some help never went astray.'

'Not a problem. I'm James,' he answered smoothly.

'Ah yes, from Jimmy's auto-motives. I've seen you around town. Good to finally meet you.'

That didn't surprise Kita. She'd lived in town for over five years and Blake had only been here for two, yet he knew more people than she did. Was probably on a first-name basis with at least half the townsfolk. She just wasn't that kind of social butterfly. Which was a shame, because, as her mother kept telling her, perhaps it was time to get out there and start meeting people again. *Get back on the horse*, as her mum put it. Kita wasn't sure she'd ever be ready to get back on the horse. She'd never be ready to move on from Will. How could you move on from someone who was the love of your life? Your soulmate.

And it wasn't like she didn't have any friends in Jindabyne. There was Rachael, the quirky mother of four who ran one of the many ski-hire shops in town, along with her husband, Bradly. Kita looked forward to the nights Rachael invited her over for dinner, when she joined in their family fun, listening to the kids laugh and squabble around the table.

Then there were Sammy and Charlotte, two more women she'd met through a book club she joined with Rachael six months ago. To try and broaden their minds and their horizons, Rachel had stated when she told Kita they were both going, whether she liked it or not. Neither Sammy nor Charlotte were the kinds of friends she could ask to drive her out to a search site. Not yet anyway. But she was working on it, in her own way.

'Okay everyone, pipe down and listen up. Here comes the important stuff,' Blake bellowed over the top of everyone's heads. There was an immediate hush. 'A woman has gone missing. Ehlana Bingly went out on a horse ride early this morning from her uncle's farm and hasn't returned. She told him she'd be an hour or so, and that was six hours ago. We've just had news that the horse she was riding has returned, rider less, to the farm. So, she's out there somewhere, fallen from her horse and possibly injured or unconscious.' A quiet murmur went through the crowd.

Blake continued as if he hadn't heard the muttering. 'The uncle has given us the coordinates of where her ride was supposed to take her this morning. John and I have sorted out a search grid of the area. John will be manning the radios here, at HQ.' Blake indicated a man huddled in the back corner of the tent, surrounded by myriads of equipment. He gave a quick, serious wave. 'The people on foot patrol will be divided into two teams of eight. You'll search these areas here, and here.' Blake pointed to a map hung on the wall of the tent next to him, covered in red lines and marks.

'The two dog teams will conduct searches in these areas.' Again, he pointed to two highlighted grids on either side of the foot patrol areas. 'Everyone come and get your radios and GPS's please, then I'll answer any questions you have.'

Kita's heart jerked in her chest as she gazed at the area she and Leroy were assigned. Would they find that poor woman? Or would they at least be able to clear the area so they could move on to the next one? A human life now rested on her and Leroy's ability to work as a team. Not just on Leroy's nose and his big heart, but on their communication skills, on her ability to read the dog's body language.

Was she ready for this huge responsibility? Her hands were suddenly damp against Leroy's lead.

James

'How can I help?' James asked above the hubbub of people collecting their radios. He hadn't even been sure he was going to ask until the words left his lips. But the adrenaline and aura of urgency surging through the crowd affected him. There was nothing he needed to get home for. The dozen or so beers waiting for him in the refrigerator would still be there in a few hours.

Blake cast him an inscrutable look. 'How good are you at navigating?'

'Fair to middling,' he replied. 'I've done my share of hiking and camping in the mountains.'

'Ever used a GPS before?' Blake held up a little square gadget. Kita stood a few feet away, her head bent over her small hand-held radio, keying in the correct channel that all the search teams were using. She seemed to be studiously ignoring him, but he could tell she was listening to every word. Probably wondering why he'd volunteered so readily. Much like himself. Leroy was standing next to her, bright eyes taking in everything being said above him.

'Nope, but I'm a fast learner.' It was true. He was good with all things technical. And good with his hands, with working things out. It was one of the reasons he'd become a mechanic. Blake was still looking at him, as if sizing him up.

The scrutiny unnerved James, he wasn't sure if he'd be found wanting. But suddenly a wide grin split the older man's face.

'Great. I'll give you a quick lesson. Then you can go with Kita.'

Kita's head came up sharply at the mention of her name.

'What? Him? Why?' she asked, the questions echoing around the tent. He'd been sure he was about to be sent off with the foot patrol team or something else simple.

'Because you need a navigator. This isn't a training exercise, Kita. This is life and death.' Kita's face paled visibly at his words. 'All dog teams need a navigator when they're on a search. Remember?'

'Yes, I remember, but …'

'And we're short-staffed today. Damo couldn't make it, one of his kids fell off the trampoline and broke their arm this morning. And Sasha, well, I can't get hold of her.' Blake gave a shrug that James interpreted as acknowledgment of the young girl's unreliability. 'I'm sorry we don't have anyone experienced to be your navigator, but I was going to pull someone off the foot patrol. However, if James is as capable as he looks, then he'll do nicely.'

She opened her mouth as if about to say more, when Blake added, 'Are you equipped for an afternoon in the bush?' Blake's gaze roved over James, assessing his outfit, hand rubbing his chin as he thought out loud. 'Your coat looks serviceable. We might get rain, or even sleet this afternoon. Boots look hardy, they'll do in this rough terrain. What about water? Food? First aid gear?'

James didn't know which question to answer first. Kita was moving restlessly beside him, as if she wanted to interrupt, but wasn't sure what to say.

'I've got a backpack in the car. A bottle of water. A thermos of hot coffee. A few Tim Tam biscuits. Will that do?'

'Sounds good, I might change my mind and take you as

my navigator instead. As it is, I'll have to take Patricia, John's wife. And she's a hard task-master.' Blake slapped him on the back.

James cast a quick glance in Kita's direction. She was shooting them both a dark look from beneath lowered brows. Not a good sign. James was just as surprised as she was to be asked to do this. In the car on the way up, she'd confided this was her first real search and rescue. She hadn't admitted it, but she must be nervous.

'You okay with this, Kita?' Blake's tone was serious, but there was a mild quirk to his lips.

'Course I am, Blake.' She gave him an over-bright smile.

'Right. Here's your map and your instructions. Follow Olsen's Road for another four miles and take the fire-trail marked on the map.'

James leaned in over the top of Kita to get a better look at where Blake's finger was pointing. Kita was so small he could rest his chin on top of her head if he wanted to. Her hair smelled lightly of cinnamon. Clean and spicy. He drew the smell deep into his lungs.

'Got it,' Kita said, folding the map shut.

James took a quick step back. Why was he smelling the woman's hair, for God-sake? He'd made a vow to stay well away from women. They were all trouble. Bridget had well and truly burned a hole right through his heart. Left it smoldering and incapable of ever trusting anyone of the female persuasion again. He was a sworn bachelor from now on.

'James, over here.' Blake beckoned him to the table and gave him a quick run-down on how to use the GPS to track where they were going and where they'd been. He explained that a dog needed to track into the wind to give it the best chance to catch a scent. So he, Kita and Leroy would walk a set grid pattern back and forth across their allotted area. The

GPS would not only stop them from getting lost, but also show them where they'd been so they didn't search an area again unnecessarily. It was more complicated than James initially thought.

It took them ten minutes to drive to the fire-trail and another ten minutes to negotiate their way up the winding track. It hadn't been maintained very well, the national park rangers needed to come and clear a couple of dead trees partially blocking the road, as well as cut the long grass back. Kita didn't speak for the whole drive, and James wondered if she was composing herself for the search, or if she was silently stewing because she'd been given him as her navigator. He really hoped he didn't let her down.

'Stop here,' she said loudly. 'This is the first corner of our search area.'

He nosed the car into the long grass, as far off the road as he dared.

'I'm not sure what Blake told you, but I need you to stay well behind me while we're searching. You're really just here to make sure I don't get lost or hurt.' A tiny frown caused faint furrows in her brow. It was cute. She was cute when she was concentrating and ordering him around. He could almost forgive her for her tone when that dimple formed in her chin as she glared at him. But her gaze wasn't focused on him, it was turned inwards, and he could tell her mind was turning at a million miles an hour.

'Roger that.' He hid a smile and squashed the urge to salute her. 'Am I allowed to ask why?'

'What? Oh sorry.' Her focus returned to him and the interior of the car. 'It's so you don't muddy the scent. Leroy is trained to search an area to find a person. He doesn't necessarily know which person he's supposed to find, he'll indicate on anyone he finds in the area.'

'Okayyyy,' he replied, not a hundred percent sure what she

meant.

'Come on, I'll explain it to you as we walk. We need to get this search happening.'

Kita untied Leroy from the back of the car and shouldered her backpack. Leroy gave a few happy barks as they set off towards a large tree. James hurriedly grabbed his own backpack, the GPS and the thermos and strode after her. The bush was sparse this close to the fire-trail, but it got thicker further in, large eucalyptus trees towering above them and smaller, waist-high shrubs filling in the undergrowth between the trees. How were they going to find their way through this? Let alone keep to the straight grid lines on the map?

'Are you right to go?' Kita called back over her shoulder. When he grunted his reply, she bent down and unclipped Leroy's leash. 'Away find,' she said in a high-pitched tone, filling her voice with enthusiasm. 'Away find,' she repeated.

Leroy barked once and took off into the bush, nose up and tail waving in the air.

James fell into step behind Kita, keeping one eye on the GPS and one on her. But it seemed she didn't need him. Not yet anyway. She made her way unerringly through the scrub on her first transect.

'Lots of people get confused about the different ways we use dogs to search for lost people. Most dogs are like Leroy, they're trained to do an area search. Which means he will keep looking until he finds someone. It doesn't have to be a specific person, it's just the first person he finds. It's the reason we keep the foot patrol separate from the dog search areas. So the dogs don't get confused. Then there are tracking dogs. They're taught to follow the trail of a specific person. A lot of police dogs are tracking dogs. They might be given a scent item, a personal belonging, like a piece of clothing. Or they might be shown to the very beginning of the trail, the spot where the person was last seen, and they can pick the trail up that way.'

'You're right, I thought all dogs tracked, like what you see on TV and on the cop shows.'

'We don't have any tracking dogs working in this team at the moment. Blake is training Rusty to track and he's doing really well. But it'll be a few more months before he's ready.' Kita turned her intense gaze on him before quickly returning it to her dog, who was now nearly fifty meters in front of them, winding through the thickening scrub. Now James understood why the dog wore a bell and a light on his jacket. Leroy might become invisible in this thick undergrowth, but at least they could still hear him.

He let Kita find a pathway through the encompassing trees and he followed closely behind. She'd pulled a woolen knit hat on, hiding her long dark hair. She was nearly swallowed up by the bulky coveralls and coat, looking like a child in adult clothing. Except for the grim determination on her face. An intriguing woman in so many ways. What was her story? She didn't seem to have a man in her life. Or if she did, where was he when she needed him? There was an air of vulnerability around her. But also a glint in her almond-shaped eyes that told him she didn't like to be messed with. She was so petite, thin and willowy. The exact opposite to Bridget, who was tall and curvy. Which was a good thing.

And perhaps it was a good thing he was noticing another woman for once. It meant his libido hadn't been totally fried by his ex-wife. Was there hope for him after all? Nope, he'd sworn he was a confirmed bachelor.

His breath came out in a white mist. It was cold up here. Colder than in town. His thoughts went out to the woman lost on the mountain. If she were lying somewhere injured and alone, she needed to be found. Soon. Low threatening clouds obscured the sun, making the day dull and gray. The warm coffee in his thermos was calling to him already, but judging by the look on Kita's face, it might be a while before they stopped for a break.

Kita

'Time to stop for a break.' James' deep voice came from behind Kita, holding a ring of authority.

Kita ignored him and kept walking. Just a few more minutes, then they could stop. They hadn't found the girl yet. Just a few more minutes.

'We've been at this for nearly two hours, we need to take a rest.' This time James planted himself directly in her path, so she couldn't ignore him. Eyes dark and serious, he stared down at her. He was tall, towered over her. And broad, with big shoulders. Strong. Dependable. The words echoed through Kita's head. Something uncurled deep in her gut as he stood there, so close she could lean in and rest her head against his chest if she wanted to. What would it feel like?

'Fine,' she snapped. 'Leroy needs a drink anyway. Not too long, mind you.'

She found a fallen log to sit on and plopped her backpack on the ground with a small grunt of relief. James had been doing a good job at keeping them on track. She wasn't sure why this surprised her, he seemed to be proficient at most things he turned his hand to. The going was difficult given the terrain. It was hard to keep their transect lines straight and parallel when they had to wind their way around a thicket of low-growing silver-leaved gums, too dense to push their way through. Not to mention the huge old Snow Gums barring their way at every turn. They were about finished this area. Soon they'd have to head back to James' car. And still no sign of the missing girl.

Whistling up Leroy, she pulled the bottle of water with the special adaptor for Leroy to drink out of from one of the cavernous pockets in her coveralls. He lapped noisily, splattering drops of water everywhere and then dropped down at her feet, grateful for the rest. She patted his silky head, letting him know he was doing a great job.

James sat beside her, pulling things out of his backpack and lining them up along the log. A packet of biscuits, Tim Tams if she wasn't mistaken, a thermos and two tin mugs as well as a couple of muesli bars. Kita's stomach rumbled and she remembered she hadn't eaten lunch. Perhaps a break was a good idea. But only a few minutes and then they needed to get back into it.

Wordlessly, he passed her a mug of steaming coffee and a biscuit. His fingers brushed hers as she took the mug and she nearly jumped at the human contact. No one had touched her in quite a while. The coffee was sweet and milky and good. Kita took a few more sips. They sat in silence, drinking their coffee and listening to the wind rattle the branches high up in the trees. Was he sitting closer than normal? Or was it just that her personal boundaries were bigger than most people's? Normally, the urge to move away would be making her fidgety and nervous, but not with James. It was almost as if her body liked him sitting this close. Accepted him.

'Leroy seems to love his job,' he commented through a mouthful of chocolaty Tim Tam.

'Yes, he does. That's why he's so good at it. Some dogs never make it this far, their hearts just aren't in it.' She cast Leroy an affectionate glance.

'You make a good team.'

'Thank you. He's like my best friend,' she joked. Then immediately wished she hadn't said it. Because it was true. Leroy was her best friend. For a while, after Will's death, Leroy was the only thing that made her want to get out of bed in the morning. Did it show on her face? How much she depended on her dog.

'No husband waiting at home then?'

As a rule, she didn't let people pry into her life. She should've deflected his question with a laugh and a change of subject. Because she was happy with who she was and how she lived her life, and it was no one else's business. She glanced at him and he met her gaze with mild curiosity. Was it her imagination, or was his question a tad too casual?

'Nope.' She didn't elaborate. Let him guess whatever he wanted. 'What about you? No wife at home?' Two could play at this game.

'Nope.' He smiled at her sideways, a cheeky glint in his eye and said nothing more.

Touché. He gave as good as he got. Oh well, at least she now confirmed what she'd suspected all along. There was no woman in his life.

Kita sighed. She really had lost the art of friendly banter, small talk. It was her own fault. Living on her own, with Rachael as her only true friend, she didn't really talk to many people. Kept telling herself she didn't need anyone.

What *had* happened to all her friends? She'd been surrounded by friends back when Will was alive. Will was such a bright, bubbly, likable man. People were drawn to his magnetic personality. He was constantly inviting work colleagues over for dinner, or being asked to friend's houses for a Sunday Barbecue. But they'd all been Will's friends. She and Will had moved to this small alpine town five years ago, when he'd been offered a job at an environmental consulting agency, helping the government develop more sustainable policies for the delicate mountain area. She'd left a lucrative job in marketing, but he loved his job so much, how could she say no to him?

Then Will was killed in a skiing accident. And her life was irrevocably changed. She allowed all those so-called *friends* to drift out of her life. But that was three years ago. Wasn't it time she made a change? Re-insert herself back into society? Perhaps she could use James as a guinea pig, practice her non-existent language skills on him. He seemed fairly understanding.

Taking a deep breath, she tried again. 'You live in that big house all by yourself? No kids, a dog, other family to share it with?'

He cast her another sideways glance. 'Nope.' His smile was grim.

Right. She frantically searched her brain for more ideas on small talk. She really did suck at this.

James sighed and put his mug of coffee carefully on the log, then seemed to take pity on her. 'I have a bitch of an ex-wife who took everything I owned, except for the house, when we divorced. She even took my dog. Thankfully we hadn't been married long enough to have kids. So, yes, I live in that big house all on my own.' His voice held an edge of bitterness he wasn't even trying to hide. Running a rough hand through his unruly blonde hair, he pulled it back into a neat man-bun at the back of his head.

'Oh,' she replied in a small voice. Not what she'd been expecting to hear. Sounded like she'd hit a sore point. 'Sorry,' she added. 'That kinda sucks. But at least you got the house. It's beautiful.'

'Yeah,' he replied, staring off into the surrounding bush, not looking at her.

'And those sculptures you make, they're amazing. You have a real talent.' She was starting to regret this conversation.

'Hmm. What about you? You got a sob story as well? Any ex's lurking in your closet?' His blue eyes locked onto hers and even though there was sarcasm in his voice, it was tempered by what seemed to be genuine interest in his gaze.

Oh damn, this little social experiment wasn't going at all how she planned. Kita drew in a deep breath.

'I'm a widow. My husband died a few years ago. In a skiing accident.' These were the words she always used when someone asked. Short and sweet, to the point. No need to mess around with sentiment or sympathy. It was simply what happened. But her hand still fluttered up, pushing hard on her chest beneath the coat, to ease the sudden stab of pain. When would it get easier? To think about Will? This was another reason why she kept away from people, so she didn't have to explain herself, or see the pity in their eyes.

'Shit. Sorry, Kita.'

'No need to be sorry.' She kept her gaze firmly fixed on Leroy lying at her feet. Enough of this baring of their souls. It was time to move on. The light was fading, the low cloud turning day into night.

'We'd better get moving. They'll probably call the search off soon,' she said. Leroy jumped up and whined as she handed the mug back to James and busied herself with her backpack.

'What? But we haven't found the missing woman yet.' James' voice rose an octave with concern.

She glanced quickly at him. 'I know, but it's the rules. They don't search at night. It's different in other countries, but in Australia that's the protocol.'

'Wow, that sounds a bit … harsh. What about the poor woman left out there in these freezing conditions?' His left eyebrow lifted in disbelief, as if he doubted her words.

'I know,' she said with a shrug. But what could they do?

Rules were rules. 'Leroy and I are more than capable of running a night search, but it's for our own safety that we're not allowed out.'

James didn't say anything more, just finished packing up his backpack and taking another look at the GPS. A frown of consternation furrowed his brow, and she wanted to explain further, to justify the SES's actions.

Instead, she asked, 'Ready?'

He took one more look at the GPS, shouldered the backpack and nodded.

'Away find,' she called out to Leroy. 'Away find.'

James

God, he was an idiot. James mentally slapped his forehead. How could he have been so stupid, so insensitive, to ask Kita that question?

It was dark, the headlights of his 4WD cutting a swathe through the thick eucalyptus forest on each side of the road. Headlights from other cars, full of volunteer searchers, were picking their way down the winding road in front of them.

As soon as he saw the look on Kita's face when he asked her about a husband he should've known. And when she'd talked so matter-of-factly about him being killed in a skiing accident, a stab of anguish and guilt went through him. James never took his gaze off the road, but out of the corner of his eye he could see Kita, huddled into the passenger seat, shoulders hunched.

He'd remembered as soon as she started talking. It'd been a big thing for the small alpine town three years ago. An experienced skier, a local, killed on one of the black runs at Thredbo. Hit a tree or something. And now he searched his memory, he recalled Kita, the newsreader hungrily reading out the details of the accident, while they flashed a photo of her devastated face out to the world. Small and diminished and destroyed, a wreck of a human being, that's how he remembered her. But still standing tall, chin up and shoulders back, confronting the paparazzi and their hurtful questions without shedding a tear. When he'd watched the news, he'd wished someone would take her in their arms and comfort her. Because even he could see that's what she needed. Instead of letting her stand there all alone.

Today, he'd felt that same insane urge, as she studiously looked at her dog, not at him. Wanted to envelop her in his arms, take some of that terrible hurt away.

The drive down the mountain toward Jindabyne was a somber one. Neither of them spoke. Disappointment and lethargy sat on James' shoulders, and he imagined Kita was feeling the same way. There'd been no sign of the woman who'd fallen off her horse. It almost made James wonder if they were searching the right area. But he wasn't going to argue with John or Blake or any of the other SES head-honchos. They'd all done this many times before, were experienced and knowledgeable. Besides, they only had the uncle's word to go on as to where the woman went for her ride.

Blake said they were going to widen the search tomorrow. Everyone at the debrief had been subdued. There was no laughter or merriment as they all gathered in the carpark. Snow was forecast for tomorrow and a possible blizzard. Blake made sure everyone would come well-prepared for all kinds of weather tomorrow. But that wasn't what was putting a frown on everyone's face. It meant the lost girl would spend a night out in the open. On her own. Alone, cold and terrified. James couldn't begin to imagine how scary that'd be.

Kita shifted in the seat next to him and her gaze flickered toward him. 'Would you like to join me for dinner? I make a mean mushroom and cheese omelette. And I've got a bottle of Barossa Valley shiraz in the cupboard, if you drink red wine.'

The offer took him completely by surprise.

'It's the least I can do, after all your help today,' she added.

He cleared his throat. 'Uh, thanks. That sounds ... nice.' Surprisingly, her suggestion did sound tempting. His fridge was a bit on the empty side. Okay, completely empty, apart from the dozen or so beers. And for some reason, he wasn't ready to go home to his equally empty house. Not after spending all afternoon with Kita. Involved in the search, doing something that mattered.

'Aren't you exhausted after this afternoon?' If she was feeling anything like him, she'd probably just want to climb into a warm bed. His legs ached from all the unaccustomed walking and there were a few blisters that'd need tending on his heels.

She flashed him a genuine grin, and he felt a stab of warmth fire through his gut. 'I would like a shower,' she admitted. 'But I need to eat, and so do you. The shower can wait.'

'I wouldn't want you to go to any trouble.'

'I've got a whole stack of free-range eggs from the lady up the road that need to be eaten. Omelettes are easy, no trouble at all. Perhaps I'll whip up a quick salad as well, while you open the wine and let it breathe.'

Some adult company might be good for a change. And the idea of not sitting at home alone, guzzling beer in front of the TV sounded almost attractive. A home cooked meal, even one as simple as eggs would be most welcome.

'Well, I guess my answer is yes then. Thank you, that'd be great. As long as you let me help. Surely I can do more than just open a bottle of wine?'

'If you like.' Her laugh rang through the cabin and his lips twitched in response. It was a nice sound. A warm sound. It made that heavy thing that always sat in the bottom of his gut loosen a little.

Kita directed James into her driveway and even through the dark he could see the place was as pretty as a picture. A small cottage perched on the edge of the lake with a neat little garden surrounded by a white picket fence.

'Nice place,' he grunted as he pulled on the park brake. Nothing like his huge mansion of a place, but then this cottage also had that homely, lived in look to it. Something his was sorely missing.

James strode around to the back of his ute and leaned in to grab his backpack. God, it was cold. He couldn't wait to get into the house. It was almost spring, but the weather was fickle in the mountains, and they could often get snowfalls into early summer.

Kita was standing on tiptoe, trying to reach Leroy's rope. She was so petite, and he had to stifle a laugh.

'I'll get it for you.' He leaned in over the top of her and reached for the knot. It wasn't until his fingers touched the rope, he realized his mistake. She stepped back to let him closer, but her shoulders collided with his chest. Her head right beneath his chin, the silken hair brushing against his neck. The cinnamon smell hit him again, just like earlier today. Spicy and warm. What did she use for her shampoo? Whatever it was, it made her smell irresistible.

'Oh, sorry,' she apologized, and ducked away under his arm as he continued to untie the excited dog. Leroy was trying to lick his face, making it hard for his fingers to find the knot and James let out a laugh. God, he missed his dog. Maybe it was time he got a new one. Because Bridget was never giving Gem back. And he missed the company, and the unconditional love that only a dog could give.

'I'll bring him,' he called out. 'I'll bring your bag as well.'

'Thanks,' she said, but seemed to hesitate. Didn't she trust him with her dog? But then she turned and headed through the white gate and down the pathway towards her front door. A light came on as she approached the door, a movement-operated spotlight, James surmised. He watched her backside as she trotted up three low steps onto the front verandah of the house. Her bulky SES coat was slung over one arm and her orange coveralls hid most of her small frame. But he still got the impression of her hips swaying from side to side as she mounted the steps and he definitely noticed her nice, pert bottom as she bent to retrieve a key from underneath the front door mat.

She held the door open for him and Leroy. 'Come on in. It's nothing like your house,' she warned.

The cottage was surprisingly warm. A quick glance showed James a neat cast-iron stove hunkered down in the far corner of the living room, glowing embers still alight inside the glass door. Kita must've stoked her fire before she went out, to keep the house warm. Another reason to be glad he wasn't going home just yet. His house was always frigid, he never bothered to set the timer for the central heating. And never bothered to light the enormous fire place that he'd once been so proud of. Always thought it was too much trouble for just one person. Maybe he should start lighting it again.

Kita bent down next to the stove and threw a few more logs in, then poked it until flames started to tickle the underside of the wood. Leroy cavorted around her while she stoked the fire, but quickly got bored and went to lie down on his dog bed with a big sigh. The poor dog was probably more knackered than he was.

The house was on the small side, but the open-plan design made if feel airy and light. Comfy cream sofas with colorful cushions filled the middle of the room, and a small table with four chairs sat in the corner nearest him. Nice.

'How are you at making a garden salad?' Kita called from the kitchen on the other side of the living area.

'I'll give anything a go.' He joined Kita as she pulled ingredients out of the fridge and stacked them on the kitchen bench. Taking the salad ingredients, he washed them and found a chopping board, while Kita handed him a bowl. Then she got to making the omelette. They worked side-by-side in the kitchen without talking. It was a comfortable silence and they moved around each other as if they'd been cooking together all their lives. Her hands were small and deft, and he enjoyed watching her chop and mix. James suddenly found himself humming. Some stupid song he'd heard on the radio this morning at the auto shop. Funny, he only hummed when he was happy.

'Ta da,' he announced a few minutes later, presenting a pretty good-looking salad, even if he said so himself.

'Thanks, James.' She gave him that wonderful laugh again, the one that threatened to melt his insides. 'Put it over on the table there, if you wouldn't mind. The red wine is in the little rack next to the table. I'm just going to get changed and then we can eat.'

Kita headed off down a corridor towards what James guessed was her bedroom. The wine rack was well stocked and he looked it over thoughtfully, before choosing the shiraz she mentioned and pulling the cork with a pop.

A few minutes later she was back, no longer wearing her bright orange coveralls, now in hip-hugging jeans and a soft, pale blue sweater. Wow. She looked … different. Amazing. The sweater set off her light amber skin, her black hair draped casually over one shoulder. Something kicked through his veins. Was it desire?

'Shall we eat?' she asked, serving the large omelette onto two plates and making her way to the table.

'Yes, ma'am,' he replied, pulling out a chair for her in a gallant swish. What the hell? Who was he trying to impress? The wine must be going to his head. Except he hadn't even had a sip. His dating skills were sorely in need of practice. But this wasn't a date. Hell, he needed to eat his dinner and then leave.

Kita

The omelette was delicious, light and fluffy and gooey with cheese. It was also nice to sit and chat with someone, not have to eat alone, like she usually did. Perhaps the food tasted better because she was sharing it with someone. Or perhaps it was just because she was starving after this afternoon's efforts. It did bother her that they were sitting here warm and dry and full of good food, while that woman was still missing out in the dark and cold. But she knew it would do her no good to dwell on it.

Kita was on her second glass of red wine. She didn't normally drink a lot of alcohol, but it was nice to be able to share that too, and it was adding a certain mellow quality to the night. How the words had come out from between her lips, she was still at a loss to explain. Before she knew what was happening, she'd asked James to dinner. He'd looked as surprised as she felt. But on the spur of the moment, it'd seemed like the right thing to do. An extension of her social experiment, perhaps.

She watched James' mouth as he talked, regaling her with a story about an apprentice mechanic he'd had a few years ago who'd got the carburetor mixed up with the starter motor. It was a nice mouth. Turned up at the corners. Full and firm. Quirking animatedly as he spoke.

James intrigued her. He'd seemed so aloof and curt when she'd first met him at the auto shop. But she was starting to learn that was just a cover. A cover for his pain and heartache. His revelations about his ex-wife swirled through her head. A few things were making sense about him. The huge big house all to himself, for instance.

Why had he joined the search today? Why had he stuck with her all afternoon, and then offered to drive her home afterwards? He'd more than fulfilled his duty by taking her up there in the first place. Because maybe he had a heart of gold hidden deep inside that gruff exterior.

'Why have we never met before?' she mused, only half-meaning to say it out loud.

'I've been wondering the same thing. Jindabyne isn't a big town.' He picked up his glass and swirled the wine around.

'I guess I've never needed my car fixed before now. And I don't get out much anyway.' Damn, she hadn't meant to say that. 'Why don't we move to the sofa, it's warmer by the fire.' She stood up, gathering the dirty plates and taking them to the kitchen. James brought the half-full bottle and both of their glasses. He was still on his first glass, she noticed. Staying sober so he could drive.

He waited for her to return from the kitchen, then handed her glass over and plopped himself casually next to her on the sofa. So close she could smell the faint hint of his aftershave. His blonde hair was out of its man-bun tonight, a little unruly from being out in bush all afternoon and Kita found her fingers wanting to comb through his tangled locks to tease them into submission.

'I'll take you up tomorrow morning, if you like?'

Surprise made her swing her head around to meet his gaze. 'You want to join the search again?'

'Yes, I need to finish what I started. I need to help find that girl.' Blue eyes bored into hers, trying to convey something.

She thought she understood. It was one of the reasons she joined the SES. To be of help. To make a difference.

'Sure. Blake was going to pick me up, but if you want to do it instead, I'm sure he'll welcome the extra help again.'

'Great.' He smiled in relief. The gentle crackle of the wood stove filled the comfortable silence as they both sipped their wine. He wasn't a big talker, but that suited Kita just fine. Leroy got up from his bed and ambled over to drop his head in her lap for a pat.

'I'm sorry I was so flippant this afternoon.' James' deep voice broke the quiet.

She brought her head up, curious as to what he meant.

'When I asked you about your husband, I never dreamed …' He ran a hand through his hair, tucking it behind his ear, which Kita was coming to realize was a sign he was agitated or unsure. 'I hope I didn't upset you by bringing it up, that's all.'

'Don't worry about it,' she started to say. After all, it wasn't his fault her husband had skied too fast down a notoriously dangerous ski run and lost control and hit a tree. Usually people's pity at her tragic loss, the fact they looked down on her—poor little Kita, her husband died and now she was an emotional wreck—made her close herself off from them. Dismiss them with a wave of her hand, as if it were all okay. Which is what she'd done to James earlier today when he'd asked. What she'd been about to do again right now. But tonight, it was different. There was compassion in his tone, not pity. Condemnation at his own stupidity, but not condemnation of her for her lack of coping skills. Maybe, just maybe, he understood a little of how she felt. His wife hadn't died, she'd left him, but in many ways, he was acting like a person experiencing grief as well.

'Thanks, James,' she said. 'It's something I have to learn to deal with. You weren't to know.'

'You must miss him,' he replied softly.

Her heart lurched in her chest. Every single day, she wanted to say. James reached out a tentative hand, his fingers resting on her forearm. The human contact shocked her. But it felt good. As if he really did understand. Her heart fluttered like a bird awakening in a cage and then quickened. His hand was warm through the soft fabric of her sweater. Firm. Magnetic.

'I do.' It was the simple truth and it made her feel lighter somehow to admit it. 'And you must miss your wife.'

'I do,' he replied. 'Well, sometimes,' he qualified with a grin. She gave him a tentative smile and his grin widened. 'Well, hardly ever, now that I think about it.'

The both laughed and Leroy whined, nosing at James' knee as if asking what was so funny. James downed the last dregs of his wine.

'I'd better go, we've got an early start in the morning.'

Kita trailed behind him as he picked up his coat from the back of a chair, gave Leroy a goodbye pat and headed for the door. With his hand on the front door handle, he said, 'Thanks for dinner. It was delicious. And thanks for the company as well.'

'You're welcome.' Now he was leaving, she suddenly didn't want him to go. She knew she needed to have a shower and jump into bed. Tomorrow was going to be another grueling day.

She leaned in to say goodnight. He smelled so good. Masculine, with a dash of red wine and aftershave. He let go of the door handle and turned.

'Drive safe.' It was a stupid thing for her to say, but it was the only thing that came to mind. That's when he lowered his head and brushed his lips along her cheek. It was a goodnight kiss. Something a friend might do. His lips were gentle on her skin, his three-day growth rasping lightly through the strands of her hair. He was so tall, he had to stoop to kiss her. Her eyes locked with his. She was ensnared within their blue depths. It was as if time stood still and she barely dared to breathe.

The thought hit her like a falling stone. Dear God, she actually wanted him to kiss her. On the lips. For the first time since Will died, she wanted a man to kiss her.

Leroy jumped up and put his paws on her arm, as if to say, *what are you doing?* and the spell was broken. James smiled and pulled back, opening the door to let in a freezing gust of wind.

'See you tomorrow,' he said, and then he was gone.

James

Dawn's light was breaking through the trees as James stomped his boots on the ground to try and get some feeling back into his toes. Today was colder than yesterday, dark grey clouds skulking across the sky. A knit cap was pulled down over his ears and he had thick gloves on, as well as a spare thermos of hot chocolate in the truck. He stifled a yawn. The mood at the early morning SES briefing was different to yesterday. The air of anticipation and adrenaline had given way to that of grim determination. No one would admit it, but hopes were fading. A night spent alone on the mountain, for someone who was possibly injured, was not good.

Kita and Leroy stood next to him, both human and dog seeming to concentrate on Blake's every word as he gave the run-down of how today's search was going to take place. They were relocating the search further around the mountain, widening it and calling in as many volunteers as they could. It'd now become apparent that the uncle had either got it wrong, or the woman had changed direction for some reason.

Blake had welcomed James this morning like an old friend, handing him the GPS with a relieved smile. There was another guy standing next to Blake when they first arrived. Kita told him it was Damo, but his dog, Parker, wasn't properly trained yet and so wasn't allowed out on searches.

But at least Damo could help Blake out by being his navigator, which seemed to please Kita.

There were tiny lines around her almond-shaped eyes this morning when she greeted him at the door. Which meant she'd slept about as well as he had. Fitfully, tossing and turning, just waiting for the alarm to go off so he could begin the day. Leroy had been so pleased to see him, he'd nearly knocked him off his feet, before Kita admonished him. Then he sat and waited like a gentleman, wagging his tail while James patted his head.

She was dressed the same as yesterday, in orange coveralls with the bulky SES coat over the top and heavy hiking boots on her feet. But now he could see beneath those bulky clothes, remembered from last night her slim, willowy form in those tight-fitting jeans. He'd meant to ask her about her ancestry last night, ask where she got her Asian looks, but got tied up talking about other things. She was stunning, with her creamy-olive complexion, smooth unlined face and dark, almost chocolate colored eyes.

Last night, after she'd made him dinner and they'd talked, really talked—a first for him in a long time—he'd wanted to kiss her. At the door as he'd been saying goodnight, she'd leaned into him, and it'd just felt right to tilt his head and kiss her on the cheek. But as soon as his lips touched her skin, a flash of desire, hot and hard, had burned through his veins. Did she want him to kiss her? She'd stilled in his arms, staring, eyes wide. He imagined her lips would taste good, lush and sweet like a ripe peach. Then Leroy jumped up between them, forcing her to take a step back.

'Ready to go?' Kita's question took him by surprise. He'd been so busy surreptitiously studying her, he'd missed Blake's final words.

'Yeah, you got the map?' He covered his embarrassment by making his tone brusque and businesslike.

'We're taking the road towards Grey Mare Hut today. It'll take us about forty-five minutes to get there. Do you know it?' Her head was bent over the dog-eared map as they walked towards his 4WD.

'No, can't say I've been there, but I'll find it on the GPS.'

'Great, let's get this show on the road.' Agitation was practically oozing off her this morning. Leroy could obviously feel it as well, as he hopped into the back of the ute without even being told, as eager as his mistress to get going.

Forty minutes later James pulled the car onto a relatively flat area beside the dirt road. The drive out here had been more difficult than yesterday, taking them up onto the side of Mt Jagungal, and he'd had to keep his focus sharp with all the twists and turns, large potholes and steep inclines. The bush was much denser than the area they'd searched yesterday, too. Which would make keeping their grid lines straight almost impossible.

The sun was up, but it was barely making a difference as the low clouds kept the day dim and foreboding. Kita was already out of the car and untying Leroy. He sat obediently as she clipped on his bright orange working jacket. If a dog could look serious, then Leroy had his serious face on. He knew what he needed to do, and he was eager to go and do it.

'You ready?' she asked.

'I'll just get my backpack.' He reached into the back tray of the ute as he heard Kita report they were in position and ready to start their grid search over her two-way radio.

'Away find,' she said to Leroy in a bright voice that belied the look on her face. 'Away find.' Leroy took off into the bush at a jog, that serious look on his doggy face. 'We have to find her today,' she muttered under her breath.

He wholeheartedly agreed with her.

* * *

'Do you want some more?' James held out the nearly empty

thermos and sloshed it around.

'No thanks.' Kita didn't look at him, instead staring out at the encroaching bush. It was early-afternoon, and this was their second rest-stop. James poured the dregs of the hot chocolate into his own mug and wrapped his fingers around it to keep them warm. The temperature had been steadily dropping since lunch time. And the wind was increasing, making the leaves rustle and groan eerily in the dim light. Even he could see there was snow on the way, without John from HQ predicting it over the radio. What would they do if it started to snow? Call off the search again?

Kita's shoulders were stooped, her gaze flat and listless. They were sitting on the tail-gate of his ute gobbling a quick snack before they were due to move on to the next search site. If they even got time to do another search area. What little light they had was fading fast.

Suddenly, Kita's radio crackled to life. 'She's been found. Repeat. Ehlana Bingly has been found. Over.'

It took a second or two before James comprehended John's words. His heart kicked hard in his chest and he let out a whoop of delight. Kita bounded off the back of the tailgate, a wide grin on her face. Before he knew what he was doing, he scooped her up in a hug of sheer elation. Thank God. Thank God. Leroy danced around them as James lifted Kita off the ground, giving little yips of excitement.

John's fuzzy voice issued from the radio again, and he put Kita gently back onto her feet. Still grinning like a maniac, she made shushing movements with her hands as she tried to make out what else John was saying.

'—Dusty, found her up near Kidman's hut. She's alive—' Loud cheers interrupted John's update as everyone else in the search tuned in. '—but she's suffering badly from hypothermia. We're sending a team to meet him at the hut. You can all make your way back to the carpark for a debrief.

Over.'

The radio became choked with people all trying to talk at once, but Kita let go of her two-way and blew out a huge breath between pursed lips.

'Oh, thank God.'

Then suddenly she was kneeling in the dirt, as if her legs were no longer able to hold her up.

'Kita, are you okay? What's wrong?' James dropped to the ground beside her.

She held up a hand and waved it feebly in the air, as if to say she was fine, but she wasn't. Tears were streaming down her face.

'It's okay, they found her,' he said, confused by her sudden change in emotions.

'I know,' she hiccupped. 'Sorry, I'm not really sure what's wrong with me.' But her sobs were getting louder even as she denied them.

Then it dawned on him. The strain of the past two days was finally catching up with her. In one swift move he enveloped her into his arms, holding her close to his chest. She'd taken the burden of finding that woman completely on her own shoulders. He should've realized how deeply it was affecting her. And now the relief of that burden was immense.

She cried and cried into his coat, and he just held her. She was small, like a tiny bird compared to his big frame. Delicate and vulnerable, but at the same time, she had an unbreakable strength running through her. The same strength that helped her survive her husband's death. He found his hand wandering to the nape of her neck, to the silken hair tied away from her face.

She finally tilted her face up toward him, cheeks lined with wet streaks, eyes red and bright with more unshed tears. And his heart tugged painfully in his chest. She was so beautiful. And so lost. So alone. He wiped the tears from her cheek with a thumb, letting it rest on the side of her face for a second.

The urge from last night, when he'd wanted to kiss her came back. Only this time it was a hundred times stronger. It was no use, he gave in. His lips touched hers, waiting for her to pull back, to withdraw from his touch. But she didn't. She gave a quiet sigh and closed her eyes, melting into his chest, welcoming his lips against hers. He'd been right, she did taste like a ripe peach, soft and delicious and warm. Everything around him faded into insignificance, the freezing air, the howling wind, the thrashing trees. There was only him and Kita. Nothing else mattered.

He explored her mouth with the tip of his tongue and her lips responded, pressing harder, asking for more. A rush of heated blood flowed through his body. His other hand burrowed beneath her coat, seeking the touch of her skin. But her orange coveralls were an impenetrable barrier and he groaned in frustration. Her hand grasped the back of his neck, fingers tangled in his hair, pulling him closer.

Something wet and cold landed on James' cheek. What the …? He pulled back in shock, then had to laugh. It was Leroy, staring at them quizzically. James had forgotten they were still kneeling on the ground and were at the perfect height for Leroy to nuzzle their faces, which he did again, this time licking Kita's cheek with his big wet tongue.

'Oh, Leroy,' Kita scolded, but she was already pushing off the ground, away from him.

Damn. But he couldn't be mad at the dog as he got up. Kita watched him from a few feet away, with dark, serious eyes. What was she thinking? Would she hate him for kissing her?

Then she smiled. It was a hesitant smile, full of surprise and confusion, but it was still a smile and he'd take it. He raised a questioning eyebrow, as she opened her mouth, wondering what she was going to say.

'That was … nice.' She pursed her lips and narrowed her

eyes, as if she were searching for the right words.

Nice? Okay, he'd take nice if that what's she was offering. He thought words like amazing, profound, remarkable might better describe their kiss, but he'd take nice. For now.

'No, it was much more than nice.' She started pacing across the dirt road. 'I mean, how do I explain it?'

'You don't have to—'

'Yes I do,' she interrupted. 'I want you to know. That was the first time I've kissed a man since my husband.'

He'd guessed as much, but he stayed quiet.

'And it was good. Better than I imagined. So good, I might even want to do it again.' Kita stopped pacing and cast him a shy glance from beneath lowered lashes. Dark, long lashes that made her eyes stand out. She took a step towards him, then another, until she was close enough for him to touch.

'That's good.' He reached out a hand and caressed her cheek. 'Because I'd like to kiss you again, too.'

Kita

Today was Wednesday. Her car was ready to be picked up. Kita's heart skittered in her chest. It meant she'd see James again.

She hadn't seen him since Sunday night, when he'd dropped her back home after the search. After he kissed her.

She'd thought long and hard about that kiss. It'd played on her mind so much that her business was suffering. She couldn't seem to concentrate, every time she sat down at her computer, her mind wandered and her legs itched to be up and moving. The client, a small business she was designing a marketing plan for, had sent more than one friendly reminder email, asking her when their package would be ready. It was extremely unprofessional for her to be this far behind on a project. She couldn't afford to lose any customers, this was her livelihood. But still she couldn't seem to focus.

Yesterday, it'd got so bad, she finally gave up, grabbed her coat and called Leroy, snapped on his lead and headed out for a walk, even though Leroy already had his customary morning walk. He didn't mind, any chance to get outside and visit all those delicious smells, run through the long grass and bark at the Magpies was a good day for Leroy. If only she could be as *in the moment* as Leroy seemed to be, just enjoy life for what it was.

They'd wandered down to the edge of the lake, where piles of slushy, dirty snow still lay in the shadows of large boulders. Left over from the blizzard that'd whipped through on Sunday night. Winters last hurrah before summer finally came.

Perching her bottom on a low boulder, Kita watched Leroy snuffle around the gravelly edge of the lake. She silently thanked the farmer who'd found the missing woman and got her up to Kidman's hut before the storm hit. That man had saved her life. Had done what she and Leroy couldn't do. Something the rest of the SES volunteers couldn't do. Blake had talked to them all after the search was called off. Telling them it was a fantastic outcome, one they'd all been praying for. He also said it was perfectly normal to feel a bit down, a bit of an anticlimax because they hadn't been the ones to find her. But that would pass and all that was important was the end result.

It wasn't the end of the search that lingered in her memory now, however, it was the feeling of James' mouth on hers. Had he just kissed her because he was overcome with joy at the news of finding the woman? Had they both been caught up in the moment, swept up by the feelings of euphoria and jubilation?

It was more than that. Much more. Or at least it was on Kita's part. Exactly how James felt about it was still to be determined. She liked James. But this wasn't merely a physical attraction, although what woman wouldn't be attracted to a Thor look-alike? Those big arms, broad shoulders, blonde hair and blue eyes. No, it was more of a silent connection. Something drawing her towards him. She hadn't felt this way since Will. Had thought she never wanted to feel this way again. That perhaps Will had been her soul mate and after he died she didn't deserve another chance at love. James had stirred the embers of a fire she assumed extinguished. But it remained alive, and now she needed to make a decision. Did she want James to stoke that fire?

She decided, sitting on the rock, with the cold wind needling through her coat, that she needed to talk to him. Needed to find out where this … thing might lead.

So, today she whistled up Leroy, clipped on his lead and headed up the road toward town. Toward Jimmy's Auto-repair shop.

There was a surprise waiting for her as she approached the shop.

The huddle of red-brick buildings was still there, as was the big warehouse where James housed the cars he was fixing. But the little building nearest the warehouse looked cleaner, brighter, as if someone had opened it up and aired it out. The thin layer of dust and grime was missing, replaced by an aura of expectancy.

There were a few large, bulky shapes arranged on the pavement outside the building and a new sign hung above the door.

On closer inspection, Kita saw they were some of James' sculptures. The ones she'd seen in his backyard. The wonderous horse was there, and the enormous snake, as well as a few smaller lizards, a crow that looked as if it were about to take flight and even a large wild-boar, with spiky nails for fur and huge silvery tusks protruding from his mouth. Leroy gave a few suspicious growls at the life-like metallic creatures and then went in for a closer sniff when they didn't magically come alive.

'Wow.' Kita went up and ran her hand over the back of the crow.

'Hello.' James' deep voice made her jump. 'Sorry, didn't mean to scare you,' he chuckled. 'What do you think?'

It was so good to see him, for a second she was lost for words. Tall and strong, blue eyes flashing in the bright sunshine. His mouth crinkled into a glorious smile as he looked at her and a wonderful feeling of lightness engulfed her. He looked different. Had he washed his greasy coveralls?

She eventually found her voice. 'You know I think they're amazing. But what are they doing out here?'

'I've set up a bit of a gallery. I thought I might try and sell some of them. They're doing me no good rusting away in my backyard, after all.'

Now Kita noticed the sign over the door in the building read, *James Harman Metal Art*. He stood beside her, feet shuffling in the dirt, almost as if he were nervously waiting for her approval.

'I thought about what you said, how they were just going to waste. And you're right. It's time to move on.'

'That's so great, James. I'm so glad you finally realized the potential of these.'

'I've already sold two,' he replied a little stiffly, as if he didn't quite believe it himself. 'I might even start up again, make a few more.' His hand traced the spine of the horse as he spoke, fingers caressing it like a lover. Kita was glad. It was a good sign. A sign that James might be ready to move on with life. Get involved with living again.

Was she prepared to do the same thing? Did she have his courage?

Her mum had phoned yesterday, still going on about when Kita was going to move back to Perth. And it was in that very instant, as her mum phrased the question, Kita knew what her answer would be. No. She wasn't moving back to Perth. Jindabyne was her home now, she just had to learn how to live here. It wouldn't be easy, but Kita could see a light at the end of the tunnel.

She would always miss Will. There'd always be a hole in her heart that only he could fill. Leroy had helped her over the huge abyss of grief when Will first died. But she'd intentionally kept herself aloof from society, from other people, because she thought she couldn't handle the pain of missing Will and trying to act like it all didn't matter. But was she ready to get involved with living again, too? Just like James? Was it finally the right time?

Yes. The answer was yes.

'Your car is ready, do you want to come and get it?' He started to walk away, toward the big warehouse.

'Yes. But, James, I want to ask you something first.' Leroy shoved his wet nose against her palm, as if to offer encouragement.

'Sure.' He stopped and turned around to face her. Light blond stubble roughened his jawline, making him even more gorgeous. Eyes the color of the sky regarded her with interest. More than just interest. There was also hunger hiding in their depths. Hunger for her. It was that look in his eyes that finally gave her the courage.

'Would you, ah …' She cleared her throat. 'Would you have dinner with me one night?'

James

Would he have dinner with her one night? It was a surprise to hear the words fall from her mouth. But it was all he could do not to yell, hell yes, in answer.

Because she'd beaten him to the punch. He'd been about to ask her the same thing. Although up until about thirty seconds ago, he'd been unsure whether she'd accept him.

'I'd like that.' He couldn't help it, a huge grin spread across his face. 'You could even come to my place. I'm a fairly good cook,' he assured her.

It was the first tentative steps towards becoming whole again. Perhaps even falling in love, although he shied away from that thought. Love was definitely on the cards. If he was going to utter those words again, then Kita was the woman to make him do it, but it was way too early to be thinking about that yet.

In two large strides, James covered the ground between them and took Kita into his arms. 'Thank you for asking. We'll take things slow, I promise.' He understood how important that was for Kita. A woman wounded by love—by the loss of love—she'd need time and space to adjust. But she'd be worth it.

He had a lot to thank Kita for. She had given him the courage to finally move on. Motivate himself. Pull himself out from under the yoke of lethargy and unhappiness his ex-wife had left behind. And now, with Kita in his arms, a hunger surged through him. To kiss her again. To get to know her intimately. Not just her body, but her mind, her every wish, every desire.

Kita stood on tiptoe and reached for his mouth, both arms going around his neck. He kissed her then, running his hands down her back to cup her bottom and pull her in closer.

Leroy barked, wanting to be included in their embrace. James smiled and let his chin rest on the top of Kita's head. It would be good to have a dog around again.

'I always knew you were a good man.' Kita laughed as she lifted her head to peer at him.

'Why's that?'

'Because Leroy said so. And Leroy's never wrong.' Her fingers lightly traced his jawbone, coming to rest at the corner of his mouth, desire flaring in her dark brown eyes.

'Thank God for Leroy,' he muttered, dipping his head to taste Kita's lips in a long, luxurious kiss.

RESCUE HIS HEART

Suzanne Cass

Nathaniel

'Have a great time,' Nathaniel called, watching Paul mount the steps into the small white bus.

Paul glanced back over his shoulder. 'Are you sure about this?' The man's normally jovial face was marred by a frown. 'It's our last day here. The conditions are going to be perfect for skiing. You should come with us.'

'Nah, I'll be fine.' Nathaniel edged away from the concern on his colleague's face. 'You guys have a blast, I'll see you this evening, when you get back.' The words, *this is something I really need to do*, hovered on his lips, but he held them back.

'Okay, if you're sure.' Paul gave him one more piercing glance before he finally turned and disappeared into the dark interior of the bus. Simone and Karly waved mittened hands at him through the back windows of the bus. Karly even blew him a kiss and Nathaniel hid a grimace. She still wasn't getting the hint. Perhaps he needed to be more forthright with her before things got out of hand. He watched as Paul, wrapped in his bulky ski gear, took a seat next to his other workmate, Tony. Then the bus crunched into gear and roared off down the long gravel driveway. Nathaniel watched as it became smaller and smaller, then turned onto the highway and sped off. None of his workmates knew much about his past. Which was the way he wanted it. He certainly hadn't told them about the ranch where he grew up. Or about Celia. Not even his closest friends back in Sydney knew about that. He was good at hedging around questions about his past, usually distracting them by talking about his time spent in New York instead.

With a heavy tread, Nathaniel turned back toward the farmhouse. It was an old colonial homestead, double-story and lovingly restored, with a curved iron roof and large open verandas running most of the way around. Karly had found the farm stay, called Raneleigh Station, offering B&B type accommodation for their trip into the mountains. Nathaniel hadn't thought much about it at the time, this three-day skiing trip up in the mountains was supposed to be a team-building thing. An annual break to help their small office bond together. Property development was a high-stress job, and the boss, Dominic decided they all needed to get away and take a few days time-out. Nathaniel had jumped at the chance to get out of the city. He got on well with everyone on his team and the company had paid for the trip, so he couldn't complain.

But what he hadn't considered until they pulled up to the homestead two days ago, was that Raneleigh was also a working farm. Complete with a thousand head of sheep as well as a stable full of horses. The farm stay ran horse safaris into the mountains in the summer, and also offered guests day-rides whenever the fancy took them. Even in the middle of winter.

Skirting the corner of the large house, Nathaniel wound his way down a path through a rose garden. In summer the roses might've been beautiful, but at the moment they were bare brown sticks reaching for the sky. Nathaniel puffed out a steamy breath. It was cold and he was glad of his thick, waterproof coat, knit-hat, woolen gloves and boots. The mountains reared up in the distance, their tops white with snow. But here in the lower hills, brown paddocks, scattered with an occasional patch of dirty snow stretched out before him.

At the edge of the garden, the stables came into view, a clay path leading him up the slight incline toward the low huddle of buildings surrounded by wooden yards. At the sight, his heartbeat quickened. How long had it been since he last set foot inside a horse yard? Nathaniel counted back and was shocked when he came up with the number. Thirteen years. Was it really that long since he left the ranch? His home in Montana.

Nathaniel's stride slackened as he got closer. He was almost level with the first horse yard now and the familiar smell drifted to him on the brisk breeze. Hay and manure. Horse sweat and dust. They were once such comforting smells, reminding him of home. Why was he doing this again? Why was he torturing himself? He should just turn around and go skiing, stop this madness and get back to his safe, secure life.

A head appeared over the top rail of the yard, warm brown eyes regarding him with equanimity. The horse snorted, moved toward Nathaniel and lowered his head. Almost without thought, Nathaniel removed his glove and his hand came up to stroke the soft hair of the horse's nose. Warm breath gusted over his fingers and rubbery lips explored his palm. When the horse found no treat hidden in Nathaniel's hand, he lowered his head even further, shoving his forehead against Nathaniel's palm.

Nathaniel laughed. 'Is that the spot then?' he murmured as he scratched the animal right between the eyes. Never letting his fingers stop their rubbing, he ran his gaze over the horse. From what he could see beneath the heavy horse blanket, the animal was a rich dark brown, with darker mane and tail. The bay was tall, at least sixteen hands high, with intelligent eyes and a glossy coat. Someone cared for him and Nathaniel's chest expanded at the sight of such a healthy specimen.

The horse's ears flicked backward just as Nathaniel became aware of the scrunch of boots on gravel. He turned in time to see the shape of a diminutive woman rounding the corner, arms full with a saddle and bridle, just before she barreled into him.

He put up his hands and managed to grab her shoulders to steady them both. She gave him a startled glance.

'Oh, I'm so sorry,' she apologized as she teetered, struggling to keep her footing with the heavy saddle in her arms. He held her tighter, noticing how he towered over her. He caught a trace of a light floral scent as her long dark ponytail lifted in the cold breeze. Once he was sure she was steady on her feet, he let go and took a step backward.

'Thanks,' she muttered. 'I wasn't looking where I was going.'

Nathaniel covered a snort as she stated the obvious.

'You must be, Nathaniel? You booked a day-ride?'

'Yep,' he answered laconically. Something about the woman seemed familiar. Where had he seen her before?

'I'm Molly, I'll be taking you out.' Brown eyes flicked up and down the length of him. Warm brown eyes, the color of his favorite espresso coffee.

'I see you've already met George. He's going to be your mount. The owner, Rob said you're a good rider. Is that right?' She eyed him critically, as if she didn't quite believe it.

'Yes, I can ride well.' He did a good job of keeping the amused smile off his face. He could probably outride anyone on this farm, but he wasn't going to tell her that.

'Good, well George will be perfect for you then. Responsive and quick, but also even-tempered and bomb-proof.'

'Bomb-proof?'

'Doesn't spook easily.'

'Ah, right.'

Molly bustled past him and placed the saddle on the top railing, then let herself into the yard, crooning to the horse as she went. The bay gave a whicker and went straight up to her, bumping her gently in the chest with his nose as she ran an expert hand down his glossy neck.

Nathaniel took the chance to take a better look as she unbuckled the blanket and pulled it off, hanging it over the rail beside the saddle. She was tiny, the top her head only reached his shoulder. Fine-boned and slim, filling out her pair of blue jeans nicely in all the right places. He could still appreciate a good-looking woman, even if he had sworn off long-term commitments. Now that he could see her from a distance it suddenly hit him. He *had* seen her somewhere before.

'You're the waitress from the pub,' he blurted out before he could stop himself. His group had decided to have dinner at the local pub in the town of Adaminaby the night before last. Molly had been their waitress. He hadn't recognized her at first because of the jeans and large coat covering her figure. Her hair had been left to flow, long and dark over her shoulders the other night, unlike now where it was pulled back into a severe ponytail. But it was definitely her.

She turned around to stare at him, and he could see a flicker of recognition pass through her otherwise inscrutable eyes. 'Yep,' she confirmed, then went back to running long, smooth strokes with a brush over the horse's withers and down his back.

Interesting, she worked two jobs. But why should he be surprised? This farm-hand job probably paid a pittance. She obviously loved horses, perhaps that's why she did it.

Molly

Molly glanced up through lowered lashes at the man standing outside the fence. He was tall. And handsome. A city-bloke. That much was obvious by his expensive, barely-used coat and brand-new boots. She hadn't recognized him at first, but when he mentioned it, she remembered him from the pub. He'd been there with a group of people. They'd all been drunk and rowdy. But Nathaniel had been courteous toward her. His eyes had sparkled and he'd even flirted a little, touching her hand as she laid his plate on the table, and giving her a large tip as he apologized for his friends. She'd gone back to work and forgotten about him. The pub had been busy for a Thursday night and she was run off her feet. Besides, she needed that job, she couldn't be caught fraternizing with the guests. The money from her waitressing was going to help her achieve her dream. And she was getting so close now. Plus, it paid the food for her two horses.

'Can I give you a hand?' Nathaniel gazed at her over the top of the fence. There was a twang to his speech. American, if she wasn't mistaken. Americans were all charming and smooth. Loud and sometimes obnoxious. Well, all the tourists she'd met so far had been anyway. There was no reason to think he would be any different.

'Sure. Can you bring the saddle over for me,' she replied,

giving George one last sweep with the brush before balancing it on top of a round fence-post and picking up the bridle. George didn't like taking the bit into his mouth. And she couldn't really blame him, the metal was cold and hard, especially on a day like today, with possible snow on the horizon. But she had a trick up her sleeve. A sugar cube in the palm of her hand distracted George long enough for her to slip the bit into his mouth and the bridle over his ears before he had time to argue. He shook his head, irritated, but the bridle was on now and he snorted his contempt.

'That's a good ruse,' Nathaniel said, and she jumped, not realizing he was quite so close. Surprised he'd even noticed her diversion method, she reassessed his knowledge of horses. To test her theory, she stepped back and motioned for him to place the saddle on George's back. She watched with a shrewd gaze as he positioned the saddle-blanket and then dropped the heavy western saddle over the top, flicking the girth expertly out of the way as he did so. Then he leaned down, pulled the girth through and cinched it tight without a second thought. Yep, he knew his way around horses. Perhaps he *had* been telling the truth after all. Which boded well for her. It meant this ride would be much easier if she didn't have to worry about taking out a beginner. Guests often lied about their riding experience. To their detriment as well as hers.

She gathered up the horse blanket and brush and held the gate open for him to lead the big bay horse out. 'Follow me, I've got to saddle up my mount and then we'll be off.' Her Palomino mare, Blanca was in the end stable and she led Nathaniel and George into the dim interior of the building. It was slightly warmer in here, but only because the biting wind was blocked by the wooden walls.

'Where did you learn to ride?' she asked conversationally.

'Ah …' His voice was gruff and he hesitated for so long

Molly thought he wasn't going to answer. 'My family own a ranch in the US. In Montana. I was riding almost before I could walk.'

Well that explained his total ease and proficiency around horses. But why didn't he want to talk about it? His words had been short and stilted, his tone blank as if it was of no consequence.

'That sounds like my idea of heaven. Montana is Big Sky Country, isn't it? I'd love to visit one day.'

'Yes … it is.' Again, he hesitated and again she wondered what he'd left behind in Montana that bothered him so much. 'I didn't think people outside Montana knew that term, Big Sky Country.'

She was still walking in front of him, so she couldn't see his face, but his voice took on a wistful tone and she imagined his features may have even softened as he spoke.

'But you're right, it is heaven over there. The mountains, the wide-open spaces, the endless blue sky. And I do miss it sometimes.' He sounded confused, as if he hadn't realized himself how much he missed it. Until now. 'Although, you could say the same about this country too.'

'Yes, you could,' she agreed. And truth be told, even though she said she'd like to visit Montana one day, she couldn't really see herself being anywhere else but here, in the Snowy Mountains of Australia. This was the true heaven on earth. This was where her heart resided, in the rocky bluffs and cliffs of the mountains. In the icy cold water of the burbling mountain streams. In the endless green of the eucalyptus forests, marching away on a carpet of rolling hills. This was where she was born, and this was where she would live out her days until the end.

Soon, she would get back what rightfully belonged to her. Another month, maybe less, and she'd be able to buy back her family property. Which should never have been sold in the first place. She was determined to get it back before she turned thirty. And that birthday was getting closer every day, but so her goal.

'What about you, where did you learn to ride?' Nathaniel's voice broke her reverie and she quickened her pace toward the end of the stable. Blanca had her head over the top of the stall-door, watching them with anticipation. Before she answered, Molly took a quick detour, placing George's rug and the brush on a bench just inside the tack-room and picking up Blanca's saddle and bridle from a long wooden bar. The bar ran around three sides of the large tack room and held around thirty saddles, enough for all the horses they kept at Raneleigh. Most of them were out in the second paddock, taking a much-needed break from the constant trail-rides they ran during the warmer months.

She gave Nathaniel a bright smile as she re-emerged from the side door. 'Similar story to you. I was brought up on a farm nearby. I learned to ride before I could walk as well. My dad said my first word was *horse*. He said if I was ever missing, he always knew where to find me. Down at the stables with my precious animals.'

He laughed at her story and she grinned along with him, hiding the stab of pain that shot through her chest at the mention of her father.

Cooing mindless words of comfort, she let herself into Blanca's stall and rested her forehead against the horse's warm neck for a second.

'She's gorgeous. Is she a Palomino? It's hard to tell underneath that blanket.' Nathaniel came up and leant his forearms on the top of the half-door, casting practiced eyes over the mare. George stood behind him, ears pricked forward, listening to their conversation.

Molly spoke as she undid the blanket and pulled it over Blanca's rump. 'Yes, she's also a registered quarter horse. I've had her since she was a filly.' She couldn't keep the pride out of her voice. A lot rested on the shoulders of her beloved horse. Blanca was going to be the foundation of her quarter horse stud. Soon. Very soon, she'd be able to start.

'Hmm, very pretty. We had a few quarter horses on the ranch, but we mainly used thoroughbreds. I had a big paint horse, called Sonny. He was such a funny horse, I remember one day when me and Celi—' Nathaniel stopped talking and Molly glanced up to see a pained expression cross his features. It was there for a fleeting instant before he turned away, pretending to pat George. 'Doesn't matter, that was long ago in the past. I'll go wait outside for you.' Before she could utter a word, he led the big bay at a fast walk toward the large open door at the end.

Well, that was interesting. She didn't like to admit it, but Nathaniel intrigued her. Partly because of his broad, square shoulders and thatch of curly dark hair. Men with curly hair were a special weakness of hers. Or perhaps it was the way he stalked down the interior of the stables, a man of determination and vigor. Hints of the tough mountain man he'd once been still visible, even though he tried to hide it under the patina of a city slicker. Or was it the story he wasn't telling her, concealed beneath that easy smile? The pain she'd seen, if only for an instant. There was a lot more to him, that much was obvious.

Normally she tried not to pay too much attention to the day-riders. They were here and gone before you knew it. Of course she was friendly and professional toward them. It was her job to make sure they enjoyed their day. It wasn't often she took out a single rider on their own, however, and it meant she'd have to engage with him more than she normally did. Was that going to be a good thing, or a bad thing with this man? Only time would tell.

With a quiet sigh she gave Blanca a quick once-over with

the brush and hurried to saddle her up. Nathaniel was waiting for her out in the cold morning.

Nathaniel

'Who would've thought bread and cheese could taste so good.' Nathaniel sighed and patted his stomach as he rested his back up against a boulder.

'It's gourmet cheese and homemade bread, I'll have you know,' Molly replied with mock outrage. She leaned forward and pushed a stick further into the small campfire, lifting the lid on the billy to see if it was boiling yet. They'd stopped for lunch in a high, grassy clearing, half-way up the side of Mount Jagungal. Molly had tied up the reins of the two horses and they'd dropped their heads to graze on the green winter grass. Then she'd pulled a picnic for two out of her saddlebags, laying it out on a cute little blanket. It was a Ploughman's lunch, she'd told him. Fresh bread, cheese, pickles, relish, cold cuts of meat and fruit. It was delicious. And the view was spectacular, looking back over the graduating hills they'd ridden though this morning. He was looking forward to the hot tea, however. Now they'd stopped moving the cold was beginning to seep through his thick coat. The blue sky from this morning was now overcast, with low clouds hanging close on the horizon.

'I guess I'd forgotten how good food tastes out in the wilderness. When you've worked up an appetite, everything is so much better.' How true it was. For thirteen years he'd determinedly buried all memories of his past and his family. Made himself forget how much he missed breathing in the crisp country air, enjoyed riding through the woodland, a horse easy and responsive between his knees.

When he'd seen the horses in the paddock on the first day at Raneleigh, something inside him had shifted. An urgent need to ride again had engulfed him. Deep down, he knew it wasn't the animals that were his problem. They'd never been to blame. He'd managed to avoid anything to do with horses up till now, buried himself in the city, immersed himself into the professional lifestyle. His job as a property developer only helped to enhance his city-boy image.

But once he saw the horses, he couldn't rid himself of the idea if he got back in the saddle, as the old saying went, he might finally find some peace. Banish the demons once and for all. It was worth a try. So he'd followed his compulsion and given up a day of skiing with his workmates to go riding in the mountains instead. They probably thought he was a little crazy, he'd come up with some excuse to give them tonight when he saw them again at dinner.

'We certainly worked up a hunger,' she agreed. 'You'll be sore tomorrow if you haven't ridden for a while.'

Nathaniel flashed her a grin. He could already feel his calves and thighs beginning to tighten up after the long hours in the saddle. But it was worth it, because he'd been right. Back at the stables, it'd taken all his will-power to force his leg up and put his foot in the stirrup. Molly had glanced more than once at him as he stood holding George's reins in one hand, his other resting on the pommel of the big western saddle, hesitating. So he gritted his teeth and swung his leg up and over and settled into the saddle in one fluid motion. In that instant, it all came flooding back to him. The feel of leather beneath his jeans, the slide of the reins through his hands as George stretched his neck, the gentle rise and fall of the horse's hindquarters as they took off at a walk. And the way he sat, tall and casual in the saddle as the animal moved beneath him. At first he'd clenched his knees, hunched his shoulders. But George was exactly as Molly described him. Gentle, yet responsive. Eager to please and nimble on his feet. With a calm demeanor which slowly imbued Nathaniel with a sense of comfort. After that first few minutes, Nathaniel started to enjoy the ride, take in the scenery and talk casually with Molly.

The sight of Molly, sitting on her Palomino, Akubra hat pulled down over her eyes was also a good distraction from his self-preoccupation. Watching her ignited a small flame in Nathaniel's chest. She was so at ease out here, natural and free. It made her even more beautiful. Small, competent hands on the reins, lithe legs wrapped around the horse's ribs. Cheeks pink and alive with the cold and exertion from riding. He wanted to reach out and touch her, take some of that freedom and beauty for himself. The sight of her tugged at heartstrings he thought long severed and redundant.

'You said you were brought up on a ranch.' Molly lifted the lid on the billy and threw in a handful of black tea leaves, dragging his mind back to the clearing. 'So what happened? Why did you stop riding?'

Nathaniel's heart lurched at her question, the bread and cheese suddenly became a cold lump in his stomach. He watched the tea leaves swirl in the water.

'I moved to New York when I was twenty. Got a job in a property development company. And then I moved to Sydney a few years later with the same company and I've been there for over ten years now. I guess I got busy and never found the time. You know how it is?' He lifted one shoulder in a nonchalant shrug.

Molly gave him an odd sideways glance, but then her face cleared and her normal cheery demeanor was back. 'Don't you miss it? The ranch, I mean? And your family? Do you ever go back?' Her warm brown eyes were fixed on him and he shifted uncomfortably. It was stupid, but it was as if she could see right into him, down to the truth of the matter. The truth he withheld from his friends. To the lies he told to himself.

Indignation replaced discomfort as he struggled to find the answers. Just because she was gorgeous and they'd had a nice morning together, companionably chatting about harmless things as they rode, didn't mean she had the right to intrude on his past. It was private, and that was the way it was going to stay.

He opened his mouth, unsure of what he was going to say, when muffled static broke the silence. Molly grimaced in apology and fumbled in one of the pockets of her coat.

It was hard to make out the words, but Nathaniel thought he heard a disembodied voice say, 'Raneleigh to Rider One, do you copy? Over.'

The voice repeated the question before Molly finally dug a compact two-way-radio out of depths of her coat and pushed the send button.

'Yes, Raneleigh, I read you. Is everything all right? Over.' The worried frown hovering on her forehead told him everything her words didn't. As they'd been leaving the stockyards, she'd given him a general safety run-down. She wanted to make sure he knew she always carried a radio, in case of emergency.

'What's your position, Rider One? Over.' the crackly voice asked.

Molly glanced quickly at Nathaniel, then replied, 'About a quarter-way up Mount Jagungal, in Paddy's clearing. Over.'

'We've had a report a girl has gone missing on Mount Jagungal. State Emergency Services are mobilizing as we speak. They're setting up their operations down near the town of Dandang. Over.'

Nathaniel's heart stopped beating and he froze as if the blood in his veins had turned to ice. No, this couldn't be happening. He wanted to get up, move away from the conversation, but he was glued to the spot. Memories swirled, forced to the surface by the words coming from the two-way radio.

The voice continued, 'The SES say she was heading to the western side of the mountain. She was on horse-back, and she was alone. You're a bit out of the general search area. But you could still take a look in case she went further than they estimated. What do you think? It's up to you. And your customer. Over?'

A feeling of déjà vu descended over Nathaniel, dragging him back to the ranch, thirteen years ago. His pulse was erratic and fast in his throat, and he pulled at his collar, which was suddenly too tight.

'I'll ask my rider. Over,' said Molly into the radio. Fixing him with a troubled stare, she said, 'I guess you heard all that. What do you th—'

Nathaniel got to his feet and stumbled away from Molly and their picnic blanket. Down the grassy slope toward the two grazing horses.

'Nathaniel?'

He heard her concerned voice but didn't turn around. He was supposed to be out here to help clear the demons from his mind. Not bring them all screaming back down on top of him. This couldn't be happening. Not now. Not this long afterward. It was a dream. He was going to wake up and find he was lying in bed back at Raneleigh, and his mind had concocted this sick dream to torment him.

'Nathaniel. What's the matter?' Molly's voice came from right behind him, she must've followed him down the hill.

He sucked in a fortifying breath of cold mountain air and

turned around. 'I'm sorry, but I don't think it's a good idea. To join the search.'

Confusion clouded her brown eyes.

'I think we should head back to the farm.'

'Okay,' she replied evenly. 'You're the customer and of course I'll do whatever you like.'

He could feel the *but* coming. And he knew he was being unreasonable, but what else could he say. He couldn't do it again. Search for a missing girl lost in the mountains. It would bring back too many memories. Memories of Celia. He'd been so young and so sure no harm could befall him. Or her. Absolutely sure they'd find her. Alive.

Molly was still staring at him, no doubt wondering at her best course of action. She'd think he was weak, lily-livered, had a delicate constitution. Or maybe she thought he was a self-centered pig, who only cared about himself and his own luxuries, didn't give a damn about some poor lost girl. A man hardened by city-life and dealing with big business, who was prepared to leave a woman to freeze alone on the side of the mountain.

That wasn't it at all, but how could he tell her the truth? That he'd been responsible for another girl's death on another lonely mountain in Montana.

Molly

'Are you sure you're okay? You look a little ...' She was going to say crazy, but he probably wouldn't appreciate it. What was going on here? The cool, calm, discerning man she'd taken out riding this morning had vanished. Replaced by a man who seemed suddenly agitated and distressed. But what had upset him so much?

'I'm fine.' He pulled his knit-hat off and ran a hand through his wonderful curly hair, leaving a dark tuft sticking up in its wake. But he didn't seem to notice. 'Sorry, that message caught me unaware, that's all. I just need a minute.'

'Sure,' she replied. 'We don't have to take part in this search. We can return straight home if you like.' Her finger still hovered over the send button on the radio. Rob, her boss, was going to want an answer soon. What was she going to tell him? That she had a customer who was throwing a man-sized tantrum and the SES would have to cope without them? Nathaniel had every right to demand they return to the farm, this search was purely voluntary. But what man in his right mind would leave a woman lost in the wilderness and not at least try and find her?

'Raneleigh to Rider One. Over.' The radio crackled to life again. Damn, Rob needed her answer.

'Shall I tell him we're on our way home?' she asked,

keeping her face as impassive as possible, even though inside she was screaming at him to grow some balls. But then something about the look on his face made her hesitate. Reconsider her opinion. His eyes were haunted and wild. And he looked edgy and panicked, as if he would explode if she dared to touch him. There was an internal battle going on inside him, she could see it now.

'No ... don't. Jesus Christ,' he swore. Then he squared his shoulders and lifted his chin. 'I can't leave the mountain in good faith, knowing there's someone lost out there and we might be able to help. Tell them we'll do it.'

'Right. As long as you're sure?' She still hesitated, giving him one last chance to pull out. He didn't look certain. How could he go from saying an emphatic no a few minutes ago, to agreeing with her now? It must've taken a seismological change inside his head to do that complete about-face.

'Yes, I'm sure,' he said, voice gruff. He was already gathering up George's reins and heading downhill to capture Blanca.

'Rider One to Raneleigh. Yes, we'll join the search. Give me the details. Where was the girl headed? Over.' Molly listened to Rob's instructions, cataloguing the region in her mind as he spoke. She was familiar with the mountain, they often brought riders up here. They'd need to head west around the side of the mountain. Rob told her to search the area from half-way up, all the way down to the base at the edge of the Snowy Plains and they were to stay this side of the old fence-line.

Molly calculated her position even as she spoke into the radio, confirming her instructions with Rob. There was an old track cut into the side of the ridge-line a little way up from the clearing. If they made for that, it would take them on an angle up and westward. Tipping her head, she tested the air, her eyes narrowing as she glanced at the sky, gauging the coming weather. The clouds that'd been gathering on the horizon all morning were now hanging low and threatening, obscuring the winter sun. It might rain this afternoon. The forecast said to be prepared for snow, either tonight or tomorrow. Not good weather to be conducting a search. And definitely not good weather to be lost on a mountain.

Nathaniel had nearly reached her, towing the two horses behind him. His face was set in a grim mask and he kept his shoulders hunched, as if screwing up his courage to get on with the job. Even with a scowl on his face, she couldn't help but notice he was still bloody good-looking. Pity he was a city-boy. Then she shook her head as she caught her thoughts. Who was she kidding? He was way out of her league. Besides, she had other stuff to concentrate on right now. Like building her nest egg so she could finally buy her property back. Molly bent down and quickly gathered up the remains of their picnic. Put out the small fire with the left-over tea in the billy and walked over to Blanca to shove everything back in her saddlebag.

'We've only got about four or five more hours of daylight,' she said, taking Blanca's reins from his hand. 'It'll take us around twenty minutes to get further up toward the summit and then we can start a search grid on the way down.'

Mounting up in one swift movement, she waited for him to do the same. He was still a little rusty in the saddle, she could tell he was already stiffening up from the morning ride. But the ease and familiarity was there in the way he sat, the way he used one hand to hold the reins as he clucked at George to get him moving. George liked Nathaniel as well. Ears pricked forward, he stepped lightly up the hill, eager to go wherever his rider asked him.

'The scrub can get thick and messy up there in places, and it might be slow going, so we'll stick together.' She'd really like to be able to separate, they could search a larger area that way, but she wasn't letting him out of her sight. The last thing they needed was to be looking for two lost people up on Jagungal. They rode together, stirrups nearly touching as they negotiated the steepening hillside.

He turned to regard her, face pensive. 'Okay, you're the boss. Let me know what you want.'

As he continued to stare at her, a shaft of sunlight struggled through the dense clouds, lighting up his features. Wow, why hadn't she noticed how blue his eyes were before? They were brilliant blue in the sunshine, the color of a cerulean ocean off the coast of some tropical island. She wanted to drag her gaze away, but she'd become transfixed. Nathaniel had flatly refused to wear a riding helmet when she'd offered it back at the stables. She'd tried to force it on him—Rob said they had a duty of care to their customers. But apart from declining to take him out, what else could she do when he politely but firmly spurned her offer? He said he was a good rider, had never worn one back on the ranch and wasn't about to start now. Then he pointed out she wasn't wearing one either, preferring to stick to her Akubra. He pulled a black, wool knit-hat from out of a pocket and dragged that on over his curls. It suited him. Gave him a rough, outdoorsy look. And now his blue eyes positively smoldered as he looked at her from beneath dark eyebrows. One eyebrow winged up in a question as their gazes stayed locked.

Clearing her throat, she turned to face the encroaching bush, urging Blanca to increase her pace. 'Right. Follow me. There's an old track up here, they used it to bring the cattle up to the high country back in the days when they were still allowed to graze them here.'

'Lead on,' he replied.

Was that smug amusement she heard in his tone? Had he noticed the attraction sizzling between them, or was it her overactive imagination? No more fraternization with the customers, she decided. It was time to get serious and get on with this search.

Nathaniel

Nathaniel stared out into the deepening dusk. Sounds of Molly putting the blanket on Blanca drifted to him from inside the stable. He continued to stand in the doorway and stare moodily as the last glimmer of light left the top of the mountain ridge in the distance, plunging the valley into complete darkness.

They hadn't found the lost girl. There had been no sign of her. She was still out there on the mountain somewhere. Nathaniel thumped the side of the barn with a closed fist. Goddamnit. Why couldn't they find her?

'You okay?' Molly's head appeared around the side of the large door.

'Oh, yeah,' he replied. 'Just venting a little frustration,' he added, a touch embarrassed she'd witnessed his lack of self-control.

'I'm going to switch the lights off,' she warned as the stables and surrounding yards were plunged into darkness.

He blinked a few times, adjusting his eyes to the gloom. The farmhouse stood out in a bubble of light and warmth further down the hill. He felt rather than saw Molly appear by his side.

'Give it a few seconds, you'll be able to see better soon.'

They both stood in the dark and silence together. Molly

was a small but solid presence beside him. Her head hovered around the height of his shoulder.

'Are you going to keep searching tomorrow?' he asked when the silence got too much for him to bear.

'Yes. Why?' He could hear the cautious surprise in her voice.

'I want to come with you.'

'Oh. Ah ...' Now she made her surprise obvious, even mixed it with an ounce of disbelief. Of course she'd be surprised that he wanted to keep searching, after his little act out there earlier today. He must've looked like a complete uncaring bastard when he'd first refused to join the rescue effort. But he'd been in shock, as if a thunderbolt had flashed out of the sky and knocked all the wind out of his lungs.

'I *need* to come with you,' he amended, doing a fine job of keeping his voice calm, tone even and expressionless. He wasn't going to beg. He needed her to understand he was going to join the search tomorrow, no matter what. He had to make sure that girl was found, wouldn't be able to live with himself until she was.

'Aren't you supposed to leave tomorrow?' Her head was tilted to one side and he caught the gleam of her eyes in the light from the farmhouse as she studied him.

'I'll extend my stay. For as long as it takes.'

'Riiiight.' She drew the word out as she considered him. 'Sounds like you've made up your mind.'

'Yes, I have.'

'I'll talk to Rob and let you know what he says. Of course the search is voluntary, so we can't stop you joining in. But it's unusual for a guest to make this kind of request.'

'Is it?' He wouldn't know and he didn't really care.

'Nathaniel.' Her warm hand landed on his forearm, arresting his attention. 'Is there something else going on here? Something I need to know?' The feel of her hand distracted him. The weight was comforting and made him want to trust her. But he couldn't just blurt it all out. Not here and not now.

'I can't leave until she's found. I'm not really sure how to explain it, but I feel like I owe her a debt. I'm involved now and I need to see it through to the end.' His hand came up to cover hers for a fleeting second before he moved away slightly and the mood was broken.

'I know how you feel,' she replied. 'I feel a little that way as well. Come on, this way,' she said, indicating they start walking back toward the farmhouse. They strolled amicably, side by side down the dim pathway. Then her stomach rumbled loudly in the night and they both laughed.

'I'm starving as well,' he said, patting his own empty stomach. 'Are you going to join us for dinner tonight?'

Dinner at the farm stay was a casual, loud affair, where all the guests gathered around a huge dining table next to the biggest log fireplace Nathaniel had ever seen. Even by Montana standards. Most of the staff sat at the table to eat too, joining in the banter and stories from the day's activities. Mal, the bus-driver, mechanic and general maintenance man had joined them last night at the table, along with Rob and Marge, the owners and two youngish guys who said they'd been out fixing fences all day. But Molly hadn't been there.

'No, sorry, I've got a shift at the pub tonight. I'll grab something to eat on my way out,' she replied, keeping her head down as she concentrated on negotiating the path in the dark.

'Wow, do you work there every night?' he asked, a little nonplussed.

'As many shifts as I can get. And it is Saturday, so they'll need every hand on deck. It'll be busy.'

Nathaniel could imagine the pub, crowded with farmers and locals letting their hair down after a long working week. The talk would be all about the missing girl, that much he knew.

'Why do you work two jobs?' She didn't have to answer his impertinent question, but he was intrigued. Why did she work so hard?

'I need the money,' she replied, so quietly he almost didn't catch the words.

'Got something special in mind?'

'I'm saving up. To buy a property.' In the dark, he could just make out Molly's form as she kicked a stone with her toe. 'I want to breed quarter horses.'

'Ah.' That answered a few questions, but his interest was piqued. It was a mammoth task saving up that much money on two miserly farm-hand and waitressing wages, properties around here wouldn't come cheap. 'Is Blanca going to be part of your breed stock?'

'Yep, that's the idea. I've got a quarter horse stallion agisted here as well. He's a gorgeous chestnut called Arrow. I'll let you meet him in the morning if you like?'

'Can't go past a good bit of horse-flesh,' he quipped.

Later that evening, Nathaniel stood, again staring out at the darkened paddocks, only this time through the glass window pane of the guest lounge room.

'Hey, mate, whatcha up to?' Paul slapped him on the back as he came up to stand beside Nathaniel.

'Nothing much,' he replied. He was wondering how that poor girl, lost up on the mountain was coping, alone and freezing, and he was desperate to get back out and resume the search for her. But he kept his tone light for Paul's sake.

'Tony just told me you're not coming home on the bus with us tomorrow. You're going to keep on with the search for the girl?'

'Yeah,' Nathaniel replied, turning and mustering a smile. The concerned furrow was back in the middle of Paul's forehead. While he never let his work relationships cross the boundaries into pure friendship, Nathaniel respected Paul. He worked hard and was ambitious, but he tempered those traits with a generous spirit; he genuinely cared about other people. Nathaniel knew Paul had a family, a wife and two gorgeous little daughters waiting for him at home, which kept him grounded and considerate.

'I can't leave. Not without knowing if they find that girl.' Out of everyone here, Paul would hopefully understand his need to continue.

'Right. Well, good on you. It's a fine thing you're doing. And if I didn't have a family to get home to, I'd join the search too.'

Nathaniel glanced at Paul and decided that he probably would've done exactly that. Paul really was a good guy. But Nathaniel still wasn't going to confide in him as to his deeper motives for staying. None of his mates from Sydney knew anything but the barest details of his life before he moved to the big city. Of course they'd been curious to begin with, but when Nathaniel continued to keep his answers vague, changing the topic whenever they asked, they eventually stopped with the questions. None of them even knew he was supposed to have inherited a ranch. To have taken over the family business in Montana, once his father became too old to run it. He'd heard through the grape-vine, from old friends on FaceBook back in Montana, that his younger brother, Brad had taken the reins. If things had played out differently, Nathaniel would be working with his hands, sweating and laboring out in the sunshine, riding horses everyday. Not sitting in some high-rise city office brokering million-dollar-deals for other people. Admittedly, the job had made him wealthy in his own right, wealthier than working on the ranch would've. But the money wasn't the problem.

'I don't think Karly is very impressed,' Paul muttered under his breath, so only Nathaniel could hear. 'I think she was hoping … Never mind,' he finished lamely when he noticed the look in Nathaniel's eyes.

Nathaniel knew exactly what Karly had hoped for. She'd been covertly flirting with him at work for the past six months now. He'd tried to politely show his lack of interest, but because he hadn't wanted to offend perhaps he hadn't been firm enough with her. Even if Nathaniel had been in the market for a relationship—which he usually kept short and sweet, and would never dare choose someone from work—he wouldn't have gone out with Karly. She was too … High maintenance. Always preening and posing for her Instagram photos. And a bit of a control freak, he'd noticed she was completely obsessed about what she ate—watching her weight—and her desk was always way too tidy. The complete opposite of Molly. She was pretty, beautiful actually, but in a natural, free kind of way. Molly wasn't afraid to get her hands dirty and do a hard day's work for a living. To achieve her goals. So sassy and strong, obviously loved her horses with a passion and—

Whoa, why had his thoughts suddenly turned to Molly? Paul was staring at him and he forced his mind back onto their conversation.

'I know, and I'm sorry,' Nathaniel apologized. 'I don't want to put any kind of dampener on the trip. I had a great time, Karly did a great job organizing it.'

'Well, you should go and tell her that.' Paul frowned thoughtfully in the direction of the large dining table, where Karly stared back at them, a curious lift to her eyebrow. 'Will you be back at work on Monday?'

'I bloody-well hope so,' Nathaniel growled. 'If the SES don't find that girl tomorrow …' He trailed off, not wanting to say the words, in case they came true.

'Righto then, mate.' Paul slapped him again on the back. 'I guess we'll see you at work. I hear you'll be up and gone before sparrow-fart, so we won't see you in the morning.'

'I'll come and say goodbye to everyone.' Nathaniel motioned toward the other side of the room and followed Paul back to the table. It was only fair to go and thank Karly for arranging this trip. To make polite conversation for a while. How long was long enough before he could beg off and go upstairs to his room? Get away from their frivolity and friendly banter. It was the last thing he felt like dealing with at the moment, his mind was so full of heavy foreboding, imagining how terribly dark and freezing cold it must be up on that mountain. One last time, he allowed his gaze to flick back to the view out the large picture window. But all he could see was his reflection, the looming mountain range he knew was out there, obscured by the night.

Molly

'They're forecasting snow today. Maybe even a blizzard.' Molly threw the words back over her shoulder to Nathaniel as they trotted their horses in single file through the valley. There were four of them today. The other two young stock hands from the farm stay, Patrick and Dozer, had joined the search as well. They brought up the rear, keeping their heads tucked well down into their coats to ward off the freezing wind that was slicing through them all like a knife through butter.

Nathaniel glanced up at her from beneath his knit-hat, lifting his mouth into a wry half-smile. Molly could only just make out his features. The sun wasn't quite above the horizon yet. The sky would've been blushing a subtle pink about now as dawn stole up on them, if it wasn't for the low, ominous clouds covering the sky. The SES volunteers, the foot soldiers and a couple of dog teams would be assembling on the side of Mount Jagungal, too. Ready to fan out and continue the search.

They spent the rest of the hour-long ride out to the base of the mountain with a minimum of conversation, all concentrating on getting to the start of their search area. She moved with the rhythm of her horse, glad for the activity as they trotted, and cantered when they could, to help keep some of the cold at bay.

As if Blanca could read her mind, the Palomino drew to a halt almost before Molly pulled on the reins. 'We'll split up here,' she instructed. 'Patrick and Dozer, you all set?'

'Yep, got the two-way,' Patrick replied, patting his coat pocket. 'Dozer's got the water and food.' He gave a quick sidelong glance at his mate. They didn't say much, but then they probably didn't need to. Spending many long hours in each other's company as they worked side by side made for an easy companionship. 'We'll keep in touch,' he said, wheeling his big black horse around and heading off to the left at a fast trot, Dozer right behind him.

'Just us now.'

Molly turned at the sound of Nathaniel's voice. 'Yes,' she replied. 'We've been given a revised search area. The SES suspect the missing woman might not have gone in the direction her uncle thought after all. So we're going to search further around the mountain from where we were yesterday.'

'Bloody idiots, how could they have got it so wrong?' Nathaniel cast a glance up at the top of Mount Jagungal, which nearly touched the low-hanging clouds, his dark brows drawn down in a frown. 'That girl has been missing for nearly twenty-two hours, lost in the cold and the dark and they're only now telling us we were searching in the wrong place. Fools.' His voice got louder as he spoke, and she noticed his fists clenched tightly on the reins.

'I don't think it was their fault, they can only go on the information they were given.' His hostility toward the people organizing the search seemed a little over the top. Actually, his whole demeanor, ever since they'd first heard about the lost girl, seemed a little over the top. As if he were taking it personally.

'Are you sure you want to do this? If it's upsetting you, we should—'

'No, I'm not going back to the farm. Like I said last night, I need to do this.'

'Okay.' Molly watched him for a few seconds, deciding. There was something else going on here and she needed to know what it was. Something was making him touchy and disagreeable, stretching this man's emotions to the limits.

'It's this way.' Pointing toward a slow-running creek she motioned for them to walk toward a cutting between the banks, where the ground sloped so they could walk the horses easily through the shallow water. Once they were through and up the other bank, she drew Blanca to a halt again and faced Nathaniel.

'But I'm only going to agree to keep going if you tell me what's going on. Why is this so important to you?'

Nathaniel narrowed his eyes at her, the pupils going dark and brittle, and for a second she thought he might deny anything was wrong. Spit out angry words in her face and tell her to mind her own business. Then a flash of something else —regret or relief—was there and gone in his face before she knew it.

'Alright, I'll tell you. But can we keep walking?'

'Sure, this way.' She let Blanca have her head, allowing her to pick her own way through the long grass. They needed to get to the top of the valley, then once they reached the tree-line they could start to climb the mountain-side. This time they were going to cut straight through the bush, there was no easy trail to take them where they needed to be today.

Nathaniel kept George walking alongside Blanca, so close their knees sometimes bumped gently together.

'I already told you I used to live in Montana, on a ranch.'

'Yes.' She tried to keep the impatience out of her tone. He clearly needed to tell this in his own time.

'I was involved in a search and rescue over there. A girl went missing in similar circumstances. Said she was going out for a quick ride.' He drew in a sharp breath, as if it hurt him when he spoke. 'Celia was my fiancé.'

A chill ran down Molly's spine.

'We'd only been going out for a little over six months. She moved in with me on the ranch after two months. She said that if you knew something was right then why argue with it. Right?' After that first quick show of emotion he kept his tone flat, but she could tell it was costing him dearly to say the words. 'We'd had a fight that morning, and she stormed out. Said she needed some fresh air. And I let her go. I was so mad at her. It was a stupid fight, she wanted me to set a date for the wedding, but I said I was too busy right then. I needed more time.'

Molly nodded for him to continue. She wanted him to get to the punch-line to tell her everything had ended happily ever after. That they found Celia. But the way he wouldn't meet her gaze told her a different end was in store.

'At first, I was so angry at her for taking off on one of my best horses, Sonny. That she was such a pain about the whole thing. But as the day wore on and there was no sign of her, well ... you know.'

The chill spread from her spine to her stomach and she had to fight the urge to cover her mouth. The look on his face was pure panic now, as if he'd been transported straight back to that horrible day.

'It took us four days to find her. The horse must've stumbled, taken a fall, the ground is rocky and uneven up there, treacherous if you don't know what you're doing, or if you push your horse too fast. Both she and the horse were dead. Celia broke her neck when she fell. There was nothing anyone could've done, even if we had found her in time.'

'Oh, Nathaniel.' Her words were soft in the cold mountain air. Unable to help herself, she reached out and touched him, laid a hand on his arm. Surprisingly he didn't wrench it away.

'Not many people outside my family know that story. I moved to New York soon after and then on to Australia. And I've never told anyone here what happened.'

'I'm so sorry,' she whispered. Jesus, if only she'd known, she might not have agreed to bring him with her today. What a devastating thing to happen. No wonder he'd reacted like he had yesterday when the call first came in. It all became clear to her now.

But then, in a way, this search might be good for him. Cathartic even. As long as they found the girl alive.

Nathaniel flicked a quick glance up toward her before he returned his gaze to the long grass in front of his horse's feet. His eyes were red-rimmed, and she felt her own tears prickle behind her eyelids. Jesus, he'd been carrying this terrible guilt around for so long. It must've been eating him up inside. To turn his back on his family, his home like that, her heart ached for him. She wanted to tell him it hadn't been his fault, there was nothing he could've done, but something told her he would've heard it all before, and he obviously wasn't searching for trite platitudes from her. So, she kept her thoughts to herself.

'I swore I'd never ride a horse again. It was one of my horses that killed her,' he continued.

That was a little unfair, she thought, but grief affected people in all sorts of ways, so she wasn't about to judge him.

'And working in the city, well, there aren't many stables or mountains nearby, nothing to remind me. But when I saw the stables at Raneleigh. The sight of the horses … this feeling swept over me. As if part of me had been missing for the past thirteen years. And I thought it might help, if I got back on a horse. After all this time, denying that side of myself didn't seem to be working, so I figured it couldn't make it any worse.'

'I'm glad you did. And I'm glad you trusted me to take you

out. I know this is only my opinion, and I hope it doesn't sound clichéd, but I think you did the right thing. Getting back in the saddle.'

He looked at her, and for the first time since he'd started his tale, he locked his gaze with hers. 'I think I did too.' The haunted aura hovering in his eyes receded a little. 'Horses were such a big part of my life. Then when I left the ranch. Decided never to ride again, I think I was punishing myself for Celia's death.'

Wow, he was really laying it all on the line, conveying some dark secrets she wondered if he'd ever revealed before. It was all a little overwhelming, and the last thing she'd expected to come out of his mouth. Nathaniel seemed so strong and vibrant, so sure of himself, it was amazing to think these tragic thoughts had been swirling beneath the surface all along. She'd only just met him and even though she was drawn to him on some level—he was dangerously good-looking after all—he was on all accounts still a stranger. Perhaps that's why he was confiding in her. Sometimes it was easier to bare your soul to someone you barely knew, than your closest friend.

'Maybe you were,' she admitted softly. 'But maybe it's time to stop punishing yourself.'

He reined George to a halt, staring at her. It was hard to tell what was going on behind those cobalt eyes of his and she waited for him to explode, to tell her she had no idea what she was talking about. Nathaniel tilted his head back, lifting his gaze to the sky. He let out a long stream of air through pursed lips. When he looked back at her, there was a hint of a smile playing around his lips.

'Maybe you're right.'

Nathaniel

Nathaniel shook his head in amazement. Why had he divulged his darkest secret to this girl? He hardly knew Molly. Yet there was something about her, a connection, he'd felt it the first time they met. There was empathy in her beautiful brown eyes, but not pity. Which is the one thing he hated more than anything. He never wanted to be pitied. She seemed to understand this. The thought was an interesting one.

Before he could think of anything more to say, Molly was pulling Blanca to a halt. They'd reached the tree-line. The ground sloped upwards from here, the foothills of Mount Jagungal rising sharply in front of them. Time to get serious. They *were* going to find the missing girl. They had to, there was no other choice for Nathaniel.

'Ready?' Molly asked as she pulled the brim of her hat down, her eyes disappearing into the shadows. The wind picked up and began to howl menacingly, making the leaves of the eucalyptus trees thrash to and fro. The prediction of a storm looked to be correct.

'As I'll ever be,' he replied. Let the snow and wind come, he would keep searching until he found her.

* * *

'Here, eat this, we need to keep our strength up,' Molly said as she handed Nathaniel half a cheese sandwich from within one of the deep pockets of her coat. He didn't want to eat, his stomach roiled at the thought of food. But she was right.

There was still no sign of the missing girl. His heart sat like a cold lump of lead inside his chest. They had to find her. Alive. It was now early-afternoon, they only had another four hours of daylight left.

'Come on, we have to keep moving,' he said irritably as he urged George back into a walk.

'Hold up, Nathaniel. Let the horses rest for five minutes. You'll be no use to anyone if you kill the horse. Or yourself.'

He stopped but he couldn't keep his knee from jiggling with impatience as he let his horse have its head so he could graze.

Neither of them spoke for many drawn out long minutes, with only the sound of the wind—which was getting stronger by the minute—and the quiet munching of the horses breaking the silence.

Static from the two-way radio shattered the dispirited air surrounding them. 'Raneleigh to Rider One. Over.'

Molly scrabbled for the radio, dropping the rest of her sandwich on the ground in her haste. 'Rider One here. Have you got some news? Over.'

'They've found her. Repeat, they've found the missing girl.'

Was it true? He couldn't believe what he was hearing.

'A farmer, Dusty Hillman found her, she's alive, but suffering from hypothermia, so he's taking her up to Kidman's hut.'

Sweet relief flooded through Nathaniel at the words he'd been waiting to hear. Thank the Lord.

'That's great news, Rob. Over.' The relief was also clear in Molly's voice as the rigid line of her shoulders relaxed inside her large coat and a smile lit up her face.

'Yes, it's the best outcome we could've hoped for. And now you can come home. I'll let Dozer and Patrick know. Over.'

'Thanks, Rob. We'll head for home straight away, the weather is really coming in now. Over.'

Nathaniel couldn't help himself, he let out a whoop of pure joy as Molly put the radio back in her pocket. She smiled idiotically back at him, unable to hold back her own jubilation. The girl was safe. Found alive. Even if he hadn't been the one to find her, it didn't matter. His deepest nightmares hadn't come true after all. She wasn't going to die alone and freezing on the side of a mountain. He suddenly felt as light as a feather, as if freed from a cage he hadn't even known was closing in around him. The buoyant feeling made him want to do something crazy. Without thinking, he moved George up beside Molly's horse and leaned in and kissed her on the lips. It was a spontaneous thing, drawn from a deep well of bottled up emotion needing an escape. Her lips were warm and pliant. Something, a spark, a buzz of electricity, flashed between them and he wanted to leave his lips pressed to hers.

What was he doing? 'Sorry,' he said.

It's okay,' she replied, waving away his apology. 'I feel the same. It's such a big relief.' But there was something in her eyes that hadn't been there before. Confusion? Longing?

'We should save the celebrations for later. I didn't want to scare Rob, or you, when I said the weather was getting worse, but I think that blizzard they predicted is coming in fast.'

Nathaniel lifted his head and studied the clouds. They were low and very dark and now he took the time to look, menacing and full of snow waiting to fall. Living in Montana for so long, he knew a bad storm when he saw one. A few stray snowflakes swirled through the trees, beautiful and silent, heralding more to come.

'You're right, we should get going.' He gathered up

George's reins and cast one more worried glance up at the sky before he slotted his horse in behind Molly and Blanca as they headed straight down the mountain-side. 'Are we going to make it back to the farm before it hits?'

'I'm not sure,' she replied, not keeping the truth from him this time. It was going to be a long, cold, miserable ride home. But he'd ridden in bad weather back in Montana, and he could do this. He pulled the knit-hat down over his ears and urged his horse to go a little faster.

Molly

They weren't going to make it back. Snow swirled around them, getting thicker by the minute. Soon Molly wouldn't be able to see more than a few feet in front of her. Even though there were still a few hours before it got officially dark, the blizzard had obliterated everything, turning day into dusk in a few short minutes. What to do? It wasn't just herself she needed to worry about, she was responsible for Nathaniel too. If she let Blanca have her head, she could trust the horse to take them home. Horses were smart like that, instinct told them where their warm stable and bale of hay awaited.

Both horses and humans had their heads pulled in, battling against the cold snow stinging their faces. Molly tugged at the collar of her coat, trying to stop the slivers of freezing air that managed to find their way inside. A quick glance behind showed George with his nose tucked into Blanca's tail, following as close as he could, Nathaniel hunched over in the saddle, one hand holding the reins, while the other was crammed inside his coat to keep warm.

Another idea, that'd started as a small voice at the back of her mind was quickly becoming a nagging refrain loud enough to rival the wind howling around them. Should she listen to that voice? They were still over an hour away from Raneleigh.

'I've got an idea,' she shouted back to him. 'Follow me.' He nodded in reply but didn't bother to question her. Thankfully, he trusted her. They were on an old road, a rutted path really which followed a fence line. Up ahead somewhere soon, Molly knew there'd be a gate. She'd need to keep focused so as not to miss it in the thickening snowfall. Her heart gave a lurch in her chest at the thought of going through that gate. It led onto the property that'd once belonged to her father. That should belong to her. And *would* belong to her, one day.

Five minutes later, the gate appeared as a slightly darker shape in the fence, and she dismounted to undo it, disuse and rust making it hard to budge. But soon both horses were through and she mounted up and pointed Blanca in the direction she knew by heart, one she'd followed many times throughout her life.

Another ten minutes and a shadow morphed out of the all-encompassing snow. Thank God she knew this property like the back of her hand, or she might never have found this building. Dismounting, she felt along the rough wooden wall until she found the groove of a door beneath her fingertips. It wasn't locked, the door shifted slightly as she pushed it. The rusty hinges complained as she shoved her shoulder against it, but it moved. Then she was inside, the gloom engulfing her. It was quiet in here, out of the howling wind.

'Where are we?' Nathaniel's voice was muffled from where his chin was still buried in the neck of his coat.

'An old stable.'

He said nothing more as he dismounted but cast an appraising glance around the dilapidated building. It was dim inside, but there was enough light to see a series of wooden stables, four on each side, running down toward the end of the long structure, where it opened up to a large area, with an old hay loft hovering above.

'At least we're out of that damn blizzard.'

She should tell him, he deserved to know, and he'd find out later anyway. 'This property used to belong to my family.'

Nathaniel stopped undoing his horse's girth and looked up sharply.

'What?' His eyes held a keen curiosity.

'It's okay, no-one lives here now, so we're safe. Bring George down this way, and I'll explain while I turn on a light and rub the horses down.'

He did as he was asked, but she could feel his gaze boring into her back as he followed her between the stables.

When she and her father had lived here they used to keep an old kerosene lantern and some matches stored up high on a shelf in the corner next to the tack. Would it still be there? It'd been eight years since she'd last set foot in here, after all.

Handing Blanca's reins to Nathaniel to hold, she walked into the dark, feeling around with her gloved hands until she heard the clank of metal and gave a sigh. The lantern was still there. The guy who'd bought this property—more like stolen the farm from her when the bank had foreclosed—wasn't interested in doing the place up or running it as a working farm. A property developer from the city, his only aim was to break the large sheep property up into smaller chunks and sell them off. Molly gave a loud snort as she thought about the man, Tyler was his name. She'd only met him once, but that was enough. She'd hated him on sight.

With the lantern in one hand and the precious box of matches in the other, she returned to Nathaniel and the two horses, standing in the middle of the saddling area. She knelt down on the dry sawdust and held her breath, sending a small prayer skyward as she struck a match. On the third try it flared and she held it to the lantern.

'That's better,' Nathaniel said, as warm light flooded the barn. 'Doesn't look like the place is used much,' he commented, his gaze roaming over the dust and cobwebs covering everything.

'No, it's not,' Molly replied dryly. 'More's the pity.' Her throat constricted as she thought about how she'd practically lived in these stables back when her father had been alive.

'So, this is why you've been slaving over two jobs? To buy this back? It's not any old property you want then, is it?'

It hadn't taken him long to put two and two together.

'Yes. This is what I've been saving for. And I'm nearly there,' she added, chin tilted up in defiance.

'Uh huh,' he said. 'You're full of surprises, aren't you?'

She harrumphed in reply. She wasn't keeping secrets from him, if that's what he meant. She didn't go around telling everyone about her problems, that was all.

'We need to unsaddle the horses, then I'll radio in to Raneleigh to let them know we're safe.'

'Righto,' he replied, but something in his tone told her he wasn't going to drop the topic that easily.

It took them ten minutes to settle the horses comfortably in a stall and she managed to dig out some hay from the middle of the pile in the loft that still looked in edible condition for them to munch on. Rob was worried about them when she called in their position on her two-way, but he agreed it was better for them to sit tight and wait out the storm where they were. Molly was glad to hear Patrick and Dozer had made it back to the farm ten minutes earlier. They'd been closer to home when the call came in about the missing woman being found. Rob would send Patrick around with the Land Cruiser as soon as the weather cleared, but it was too dangerous to drive in these conditions.

Now she and Nathaniel needed to find a comfortable spot to settle in and try and keep warm till the blizzard blew over.

'What about up in the hay-loft?'

She startled. That's exactly what she'd been thinking.

'Good idea. After you,' she said, indicating the ladder

leading up to the hay-loft above. She couldn't help casting an appreciative glance upward as he mounted the ladder and she was awarded the sight of his masculine jean-clad ass filling her view. It was definitely a nice ass.

A little shiver ran through her as she remembered the feel of his lips on hers. It'd been a spontaneous kiss, born in the heat of the moment, they were both overjoyed at the news the girl had been found. But still … It had been nice. More than nice. Delicious. Her lips had tingled for many minutes afterward from his touch. She'd kissed more than her fair share of men and some of them had been nice, too. But Nathaniel had awakened something in her. A need, a hunger she'd almost forgotten about. Until now. It'd been a while since her last serious relationship, she was too busy working, and men required too much energy. But she was about to spend at least the next few hours, perhaps even the whole night with him. Alone. The thought had her feeling all hot and unsettled.

Nathaniel

Nathaniel sneezed and shifted around in the hay. It wasn't nearly as comfortable as it looked. Rather, it was spiky and dusty and a stray stalk had become lodged in his collar and was now itching like crazy.

He watched Molly put the lantern on a sturdy box in the corner, away from all that flammable hay. Her long ponytail fell over her shoulder and she brushed it back. He caught her profile, fine cheekbones and full pouting lips lit from beneath by the soft light of the lantern. Long dark eyelashes, the same deep auburn as her hair, fluttered against her cheeks. She was gorgeous. And tantalizing. Then she turned and made her way toward him, but seemed to hesitate as she caught sight of him. He'd carved a large hole into the hay, a kind of nest, big enough for two people to share, and now he patted the dusty hay beside him, inviting her to come sit with him. Would she do it? It made sense for them to share the space, combine their warmth. But it'd also mean they'd have to lie close together. A bolt of fire shot through him at the idea of sharing body heat with Molly. *Whoa, slow down*. This was not what tonight was about. They were practically strangers, trying to stay warm together, that was all.

So why did he want her so badly?

'Oh … ah, I guess that's a good idea,' she said, still

hesitating. 'It is only going to get colder.'

'I've brought the left-over food up,' he said, pointing at the small pile that contained two muesli bars, an apple and a bag of nuts, along with their water canteens. Not much, but he hoped it might be enough to entice her into his little nest.

'I am hungry,' she admitted as she shuffled through the hay and came to sit by him. He held back a smile at the thought his little plan had worked, instead handing her one of the muesli bars, unwrapping his at the same time.

'So, are you going to tell me your story now? Why do you need to buy back your own property?'

Rubbing her hands together, she blew on her fingers, trying to get them warm. Then she cast him a sideways glance and grimaced. 'Being in property development yourself, I'm sure you've heard the same sob story a hundred times already from people in my situation.' He flinched at the heat behind her words, but decided not to take her sarcasm personally, letting her continue without interruption. 'My father died suddenly and left unpaid debts that I couldn't cover. So the bank took the land. And sold it to some bloodsucking property developer for less than half of what it was worth.' He could tell she was trying to keep her voice deadpan, as if none of what she was telling him mattered. But he knew different, it was in the slight wrinkle between her eyes, the way she pursed her lips. 'I've watched Tyler, the bloodsucker, slowly divide it up and sell it off piece by piece.'

At least he now knew why she'd given him such a dirty look when he'd first told her what he did for a living. But he had to hand it to her, she hadn't seemed to hold it against him.

'I know Tyler has been holding back on selling the farmhouse and the surrounding buildings because he has some stupid idea of turning it into a luxury mountain-stay resort. But property prices are still low, because of the drought and other economic problems. I've heard rumors he's getting sick of waiting for things to pick up and he might be about to sell and move on. And when he does, I'll be ready to pounce.' Molly's eyes glowed in the lamplight with a fervent hope. He admired her intrepid nature, her determination to get back what was rightfully hers. She wasn't going to let anyone, or anything stand in her way. 'I've talked to the bank, and if I can raise fifty thousand, they'll consider giving me a loan. I'm so close now.' This last sentence was said under her breath, as if she'd forgotten he was there.

'That's an admirable plan,' he said. But he withheld the other words he wanted to add. What would happen afterward, if she did manage to buy the land? Running a farm wasn't cheap. She'd need extra capital if she wanted to start a quarter horse stud. There'd be feed to buy, machinery to maintain, fences to fix. Where was that money going to come from? He didn't voice his concerns, however, but continued to listen as Molly talked about her ideas. She'd been plotting and scheming and dreaming about this for nearly eight years. The need to win back her family farm had consumed her. She was so determined and worked so hard to achieve her goal. She talked and talked, and he let her ramble. At last she seemed to run out of words and stopped, staring at the lantern, mesmerized by her own thoughts.

The wind howled through a crack in the wood paneling, reminding Nathaniel there was a dangerous blizzard outside. At the same time, Molly gave a small shiver. She was cold. And the temperature was still dropping. Thank God they'd made it inside. He'd hate to be stuck outside in this.

Perhaps it was the wrong thing to do, but before he could think it through, he shuffled toward Molly, draping an arm around her shoulder. She stiffened at his touch.

'What are you doing?' She almost growled the words.

'You're cold. We need to stay warm. Body heat is the best way.'

'Hmm.' She glared at him and then tried to hide another shiver that shook her body.

He cocked a rakish eyebrow but said nothing, letting her decide.

'Fine, but that's all. We're just sharing body heat. Okay.'

'Yep.'

She relaxed beneath his arm and even snuggled in a little closer, bringing her legs up to rest against his. The feel of her lying next to him sent a different kind of shiver through him.

'Thank the Lord that poor woman isn't still lost out there in this snow,' she mumbled into the front of his jacket, where she was now curled in the crook of his shoulder.

'You read my mind,' he replied, easing himself down in the straw, finding a more comfortable position, draping his other arm around Molly to pull her in even closer. It was working, her shivering was starting to subside. Her body was soft against his, but also firm in all the right places. Heat was again building inside him too, the warmth began to pool in his stomach, then trickle lower until the front of his jeans suddenly became uncomfortably tight. This wouldn't do. He needed to get his libido under control, otherwise it was going to be a long night.

'I'm sorry about the … Well you know, the kiss. I got carried away when we heard the news.' He wasn't really sorry at all, but he was curious as to her reply.

'That's okay, we were both caught up in the moment.'

Interesting, she wasn't blaming him for the kiss. Had even enjoyed it, if he were reading her tone correctly.

'I mean, it must've been such a relief for you. The fact that she was found. Alive,' Molly said.

'Yes, it was. I can't tell you how much it meant to me.'

'I was worried about you,' she admitted, lifting her head to look into his face. 'Worried what might happen if … well, you know.'

Yes, he did know. She meant if the girl had been found dead. He hadn't allowed himself to dwell on that detail. The only reality he would believe in was that they find her alive. The alternative had been unthinkable. If she had died out there on the mountain, then the loss of another woman might have pushed him over the edge. At the very least it would've pushed him further into the cage he'd created in his own mind.

'You were worried about me?'

'Yes, I wasn't sure how you'd react. I was dreading bad news, and not only for the girl's sake. For you as well. After you told me about Celia, I began to realize how much this search meant to you. As if you might gain redemption through finding this missing girl, or something.'

Nathaniel grunted. It was funny, but she'd hit the nail right on the head. Even though he hadn't realized it at the time, that was exactly what he was doing. But it was more than that. The fact they'd been able to find the girl today, had proved to him that he wasn't the bad luck omen he always thought he'd been. He hadn't been to blame for Celia's disappearance, or her death. After the news had come through on the two-way radio it was as if some invisible shackles around his heart snapped free. Now he could finally feel the sun on his face again, let the wind blow through his hair. With sudden clarity, he saw that losing Celia wasn't his fault. The horse hadn't killed her and neither had he. It was a twist of fate. The same kind of twist of fate that helped that farmer find the girl lost on this mountain today.

But it was more than just the act of helping in the search, knowing the girl had been found that gave him a change of heart. It was Molly herself. Her presence had been a balm to his soul. Had opened a crack in the armor around his dark, self-built cage. Let some light back in.

'So, you were getting ready to catch me, if I fell?' he prompted.

She blinked and then seemed to consider his words. 'I'm not sure I would've put it like that, but yes, I guess that's what I was doing.'

'Thank you, Molly. It means a lot to me.' He stared into her warm brown eyes. This was the most emotionally intimate he'd been with a woman in a long time. He'd shared his story of loss with her, and in return she'd bared her soul about the loss of her father's farm.

'I'm glad I came here,' he murmured. 'I'm glad I met you.'

Her eyes glowed in the lamplight, soft and inviting and he did the only thing possible under the circumstances. He lowered his lips to meet hers.

Molly

Nathaniel's lips tasted like chocolate and hay, warm and musky. Delectable. Enticing. Firm and masculine. Molly found herself melting against him, suddenly wanting to be closer, mold herself to him, become one together. His long legs entwined with hers as he pulled her down further into their nest of hay. She was no longer cold. His warm hand was on her face, trailing down her neck. Heat built between her thighs.

Too fast, this was happening too fast. Forcing her tongue to stop its exploration of his delicious mouth, she slowly pulled back. Her breath was coming in sharp little pants and it took her a few seconds to slow her breathing enough to be able to speak. 'Nathaniel, I …'

'It's okay,' he said softly. 'I promise you're safe with me tonight. I promise this is as far as it goes. It's way too soon, isn't it?'

'Yes, it is,' she said, nodding slowly and breathing out a sigh of relief. He got it. 'Thanks for understanding.'

'My momma brought me up right,' he said with a quick grin. 'To respect a lady.'

'Thank God for your momma.' She shot him an equally wicked smirk, but the smile slowly left her face as she stared into his wonderful blue eyes. They held her ensnared. She could drown in his eyes. There was something there, a feeling of reverence, of familiarity. As if she belonged. With him. Forever. The thought nearly stopped her heart. What was she thinking? She'd only just met this man. How could she possibly be entertaining the idea of spending the rest of her life with him? It was ridiculous.

Nathaniel pulled her in close, and she tucked her head back down onto his shoulder. His chest was solid and safe beneath her cheek. Why did he feel so right?

'Are you warm enough?'

How could she tell him she was practically burning up inside? 'Mmm hmm,' she replied, not trusting herself to say any more. The wind shrieked, sending flurries of snow knocking against the small window as if trying to break in. But here, in their little nest she was warm and safe and secure, with this man by her side. An interesting feeling, one she hadn't experienced for a while. Since the death of her father. She'd been only twenty-one when her dad passed away and since then she'd been so busy, working her two jobs, looking after her horses, planning how she was going to get her farm back, she hadn't had the time or the energy to spend on men or relationships. Had a couple of short romances earlier on, but after they both failed, she'd shrugged off any advances until the men stopped trying. Decided she was fine on her own, she didn't need anyone.

They lay, not speaking, listening to the snow and wind attacking the side of the barn, like a wild animal trying to claw its way in. While inside they were cozy and protected. Together. She didn't have to endure this alone. Her heart gave a flutter against her ribcage. A small thing but a feeling she hadn't encountered for as long as she could remember.

The rest of the night they spent talking quietly about their dreams, hopes, wishes. Sometimes she dozed lightly against his chest, the beating of his strong heart beneath her ear.

Sometimes his lips found hers and they kissed, long and luxurious, but he never let it get out of control, leaving her wanting more, tantalized by the thought of what more might be like with him. Thoughts of his body, long and lean, pressed up against hers made her shiver with need.

But finally, weak dawn light began to filter through the cracks in the walls. It was morning, and the blizzard had blown itself out. Molly lifted her head to peer out the window. The world was white and silent outside. She needed to go and check on the horses. And nature called as well. But she didn't want to move. Not yet. Not ever. Nathaniel was asleep, his wonderful dark curls falling over his forehead, his face peaceful in the shadowy morning light.

The radio crackled to life, shattering the special moment. 'Raneleigh to Rider One, are you there? Over.'

Nathaniel jerked awake with a snort as Molly reached over to retrieve the two-way, nestled next to the remains of their food. She gave him an apologetic smile as she pushed the send button.

'All good here, Rob. Over.' As she spoke she got to her feet and went to peer out of the window. A winter wonderland greeted her. Pristine snow piled in silent drifts against the side of the barn, and further out all the paddocks looked as if they were made out of soft, white marshmallow.

'I was going to send Patrick over with the car, but the roads are blocked. The snow plough hasn't been through yet. Over.'

'Don't worry, we'll ride back. We'll stick to the ridges where the snow isn't too deep. Over.' It would be fun, Blanca would love the exhilaration of the cold, sparkling snow. 'See you in an hour or so. Out.' She ended the call and looked over to find Nathaniel watching her. 'Are you okay with riding back?' she asked belatedly.

'Of course. It reminds me of home. I used to love riding through the virgin snow back in Montana.' Nathaniel got up and dusted himself off, then came over and draped an arm around her shoulder. 'Wow, it's gorgeous,' he whispered at the sight that greeted him through the window.

'Shall we go and see how the horses fared?' She was about to turn away when Nathaniel pulled her back to his side.

His blue eyes darkened as he stared at her intently. 'I haven't spent a night like that in … forever. Alone with a woman, talking and kissing. It was so …' He couldn't seem to find the words to explain what he was feeling. 'I think we have something special here.'

His words were like sweet honey and the tiny flutter she'd felt in her heart became a constant throbbing echo. Yes, it had been special. One of a kind. But what happened next? What kind of future did they have together? They were from different walks of life. He lived in the city and there was no way she was leaving the country. So how was this supposed to work?

Nathaniel

Nathaniel could hear Molly even before he entered the stables. Two loud bangs followed by a curse drifted out of the large door and down the pathway toward him. Rob had been right, Molly was mad as hell about something. Rob had been surprised to see Nathaniel standing on the doorstep of Raneleigh this morning, exactly a week after the search and rescue effort. But when Nathaniel told him he was here to see Molly, the big man's face split wide in a welcoming grin and he pointed toward the stables, sending Nathaniel on his way with a warning.

George gave a whinny of recognition and draped his head over the railing as Nathaniel drew level with the yard. He stopped to pat George. As he let his fingers linger in the warm hair of the horse's mane another loud bang erupted from the stable and Nathaniel took a fortifying breath then stepped forward. Would she be pleased to see him? Maybe not, but it was no use regretting his spur-of-the-moment decision now.

A dark shape was hunched over at the end of the stables. Molly. She turned at the sound of his feet scrunching on the dry sawdust. Recognition skittered over her face as she stood up, dusting her hands on the side of her jeans. It was all he could do to hold himself back, not to go up and take her in his arms. She looked so good, just as he remembered. Petite and willowy, but with a presence burning within her soul. A magnetic aura that drew him in.

'Hi,' he said.

'Hi.' Her gaze was wary and he could see she was holding back barely controlled anger behind her eyes. But the lift of a dark eyebrow also gave away her curiosity.

'Rob told me I'd find you here.' Why was he stating the bloody obvious? He should cut to the chase. But now he was here, he was suddenly unsure. Had he done the right thing?

'Right.' She was still staring at him, waiting for him to tell her what was going on. But the anger seemed to be subsiding and her gaze finally softened. 'It's good to see you again.' As she spoke, she took a step toward him as if she too wanted to touch him, take him in her arms. Brown eyes locked onto his and he was transported back to the hay loft, the feel of her body against his as they lay together. He hadn't imagined it. Something special happened that night. Something that needed to be explored.

'I came to see you, the morning I left. But you weren't here.' It was true, he'd run down to the stables to find her, with Mal, the driver waiting to take him back to the city already idling the bus impatiently in the driveway. But the stables had been empty, no sign of Molly, nothing to tell him where she'd gone. All the words he wanted to say to her had swirled around in his head, but were left to wither away unsaid.

Molly gave a cool nod of her head. 'A horse over on the neighboring farm got caught up in some barbed wire. It was pretty bad, they called me to go over and help them until the vet arrived.'

'I wanted to find you, to say goodbye, but the bus driver was getting irritated and I had to get back.' At the time the pull to get back to work had seemed legitimate. The paperwork would be piling up and the boss, Dominic would want to know where he'd been. He shrugged his shoulders as if that explained everything, but he knew it didn't come close.

'I left a note with Rob, with my phone number.' But he could see now he shouldn't have departed without talking to her first. Without seeing her. The last week he'd spent cooped up in the cage of an office back in the city had proved that to him. It'd been a week from hell, he'd been like a bear with a sore head, antagonizing everyone in the office until Dominic had finally told him to go home and work out whatever his problem was. But he'd been no better at home, pacing back and forth through his small high-rise apartment until he felt like he'd worn a track on the carpet. It was then, as he gazed out over the city unfolding below him, wondering what was wrong with him, wondering what the hell he was going to do with his life now, he had made a decision. And returned to the mountains.

But now he was filled with sudden trepidation. In his imagination Molly had felt the same way as he did. But now she was standing in front of him, he wasn't so sure. Throughout his life he'd always waited for the woman to make the first move, he'd never been interested enough to really want to go more than a few dates. But now he'd found a woman who mattered to him, would he be able to make the first move? He dragged in a deep, fortifying breath. It was time to lay his heart bare. Even if it scared the hell out of him. Even if she rejected him.

'I missed you,' he said softly.

'Really?' Her eyes sparkled in the winter sunlight slanting in through the stable door, rich and warm.

He took a step toward her. Then another. Was his fear and uncertainty written all over his face?

'Yes, really. I had to come back and see you.'

Her face lit up in a smile. A wonderous, heart-melting

smile. 'I missed you too.' Then she was in his arms, hands locked around his neck, kissing him. One leg came up and fastened around his knees, pulling him in as close as possible.

They kissed for a long time, lost in each other. It was everything he'd been hoping it would be. She was sexy and inviting, her supple lips wanting more of him, demanding more. At last Molly broke the kiss, pulling back to gaze at his face, her breathing heavy and uneven.

'So, what happens now?' She asked the exact question that'd been driving him crazy for the past few days.

'I'm not sure,' he said truthfully. 'But Rob also told me you were mad as a cut snake and not to come near you, or you might bite my head off.' That elicited a giggle from her. 'Do you want to tell me what's got you so worked up?'

She gave a most unladylike snort and disentangled her hands from behind his neck. Took a step away. Would she tell him? Would she let him in, like she had the other night in the hay loft? Finally, she squared her shoulders and turned back to face him. 'It's the bloody bank. I saved up the fifty thousand, like they told me to. I slaved away, hoarding and scrimping and tightening my belt to get that money.'

'Go on,' he encouraged. Nathaniel could imagine Molly, full of conviction and bravado, walking into the bank with her head held high and the light of hope in her eyes. He already suspected what was coming, and he was so mad at that bank manager he wanted to punch him in the face. But he might have a plan to combat the small-minded lender. He needed to hear it from Molly first, however.

'I went in to see the bank manager yesterday. And he refused my loan. Said I didn't have enough collateral or some such bullshit. In this climate of uncertainty and drought they didn't have enough confidence I could make my business work. Told me to come back when I had one-hundred thousand saved up. Bastard.' Her last word was a sob. 'He took away my dream, Nathaniel. Did it without even thinking. Stomped on my heart and threw it in the gutter. What am I going to do now?' She turned her face away, but not before he saw a tear slide down her cheek. 'It took me years to save up that money, I'm not sure I can do this any longer.'

'Hey, don't cry.' He gathered her back into his arms and gently tilted her chin up so he could see her eyes. 'What if I told you I might know of an investor who's looking for just the type of property you want to create? A stud farm for quarter horses.'

'What?' Molly's eyes widened in surprise, but they soon filled with scorn. She obviously thought he was joking. 'Who? Who in their right mind would want to invest in a stud farm out here?' she scoffed.

Molly

Molly couldn't believe it. Nathaniel was here. Back in her arms. Had come back for her. Had missed her. Like she'd missed him over the past week. Missed him with a soul-deep ache she'd never encountered before. Nathaniel had gone without saying goodbye, leaving his mobile number with Rob. She should've called him. Wanted to call him. But didn't know what to say. And perhaps a tiny part of her had been mad at him for not trying harder to catch up with her before he left. She hadn't had time to think when Dan's frantic call came through that morning about his horse. She'd leapt into her car and sped over there, regret playing at the edges of her mind about Nathaniel, but she couldn't leave Dan in the lurch.

Missing Nathaniel had driven her crazy, which is why she'd spontaneously decided it was time to visit the bank manager again. To try and get her life back under control. Try and get back to the normality of her world before Nathaniel had blown in like a hurricane. Get her plan to buy back her property under way. But it'd backfired big time and she was left even more bereft and desperate than before after the bank's refusal. Wondering what she was going to do now. There was no way she could spend another eight years saving up the rest of the money the bank demanded.

And now Nathaniel was here, in the flesh, making her head spin with wanting him, and talking some kind of nonsense about an investor. A way to fulfill her dream after all. It was all too much to take in.

'Me. It's me. I want to invest in your stud farm. It's time I got back to my roots. Back to the country.'

Him? What was he talking about? She shook her head in confusion.

'I have money, Molly. Most of it invested in meaningless city apartment blocks, or helping nameless companies expand their already huge empire. I want to put the money into something worthwhile. Something that has relevance for me.'

Her mind was buzzing with all his information and she struggled to understand exactly what he was saying.

'You want to help me buy back my property?' She couldn't quite believe the words that were coming out of her mouth. And she wasn't sure how she felt about it, either.

'I would be a silent partner of course. If that's what you want. No one has to know, besides the bank that I'm even involved. And I'd make sure our contract is rock solid. The money is an investment. You wouldn't lose the farm if things between us ... you know, if they didn't work out.'

She could see in his eyes he would abide by his words, if that's the way she wanted it. He meant what he said, and she respected him for that. But she could also see he yearned for more. To get his hands dirty again. To work with the horses again. But did she want him as her partner? Did she want anyone as a partner? Hadn't she been doing fine on her own? Should she accept the help he was offering? She wasn't some kind of charity case, a mere helpless woman who needed to be bailed out when the going got tough. Was that what he was suggesting? Because if it was, there was no way she'd say yes. But then again ... the chance to buy back her father's farm would be amazing. Could she really turn down an offer to help her achieve her heart's desire? She needed more information before she could make a decision. So many questions needed an answer. Which one to ask first? Was he even intending to stay here, to work with her on the farm?

'What about your family? Back in Montana. Don't you want to go back there?'

'Maybe.' He tilted his head to one side as he considered his answer. 'One day, perhaps. It's been so long now, I'm not sure what reception I'd get.'

'They're your family, of course they'd welcome you back.' But then again, how did she know, after all she had no real family. Not any more. Her father died over eight years ago, and she'd never really known her mother who'd been killed in a car accident when Molly was barely two years old. No brothers or sisters to lean on. No one really, except Rob and the staff at Raneleigh. So who was she to lecture him on family?

Nathaniel shook his head. 'Brad, my younger brother is in charge of the ranch now. Word is he's doing well, it's prospering in his hands. Dad's semi-retired. They don't need me for anything, haven't done for a long time.'

'That doesn't mean they don't miss you,' she chided softly.

'Hmm.' There was a faraway look in his eyes as he considered her words.

'Maybe it's time you contacted them. Thirteen years is a long time to go without talking to your family,' she prompted.

'I would never admit this to another soul, but you might be right.' He pulled her back into his arms and stared down at her face. 'I will. I will give them a call. Soon.' His head dipped, blue eyes darkening with desire as he went to kiss her, but she held him at bay with a hand on his chest. Much as she wanted to taste his lips again, there was so much more she needed to know.

'Okay, so now that you're considering getting in touch with your family in Montana, does that mean—'

'It doesn't change anything regarding my proposition to you. Even if I do mend my bridges where my family are concerned, I won't be moving back there. This is where I want to be. Australia is my home now. And it took you to make me see that.'

Okay, it sounded like he meant what he said. She decided to believe him. Even though she'd only known him for a week, their connection had been strong. Stronger than anything ever she'd felt. With anyone. He wouldn't lie to her, she knew it with a certainty down to her bones. Was it worth giving this a try? Worth opening her heart and letting him in, to see where it took them?

A little voice at the back of her head nagged at her to be cautious.

'It's all happening a little fast, don't you think?'

'Oh, really?' There was unguarded shock in his eyes. He didn't seem to have considered she might need time to process all he was offering. Or that she really might say no. Letting her go, he took a step back, raising his hands in the air as if in surrender. The cold air swirled around her without his arms to keep her warm. Stupidly, she missed his strong arms, wanted to fling herself back into them.

'I didn't mean to pressure you into anything. Of course you should take some time, think it over. If you don't want my money, I'll understand. But even if you won't accept me as an investor—' He stopped and drew in a sharp breath. 'Will you still let me see you? If you're not sure, we can start slow. Start dating, if that's what you'd like.'

She almost snorted at his old-fashioned term. At the same time her heart did a quick double-time beat. Was he truly here for her after all?

'You'd move away from the city? Up here?'

'Of course. I've already put a deposit on a little cottage at the edge of town.' He waved a vague hand in the direction of Adaminaby. I finally figured out that was part of my problem. Living cooped up in the city was slowly killing me. And perhaps it's what I intended, for a long time anyway. To bury myself in my work, forget about my other life. But after I met you, after I came up here and experienced living Big Sky again. Well it changed something inside me. For better or worse. It wasn't just the girl lost up on the mountain who needed rescuing. I think you saved me as well. You woke up my heart. You showed me that life is worth living again. You rescued me, Molly.'

'Oh,' Molly breathed, not trusting herself to say anything more. If it was true that she'd reignited his heart, then he'd done the same for her. Because there was a strange feeling engulfing her, as if a dam was breaking somewhere deep inside, spilling fire and ice through her veins.

Nathaniel stared at her, his eyes shining with a mixture of hope and fear.

Yes.

The word formed in her brain.

Yes.

Her body responded to the silent word, pushing her forward without conscious thought.

She took each of his hands in hers, warm even though the air was cold around them. And looked up, meeting his eyes. 'Okay, let's give it a go.'

'Really?'

'Really. Let's breed some world-class quarter horses together.'

'Thank you, Molly.' This time when he gathered her into his arms, she didn't push him away. Instead, she let his lips find hers, warm and demanding and deliciously right. She ran a hand through his dark curls, letting her fingers luxuriate in the texture. He pulled her up higher, so her feet left the ground and his strong biceps curled around her waist, holding her tight against him. It was hard to believe that this spectacular man was hers. She lost herself in the feeling of him kissing her. So passionate and genuine and real.

Suddenly, her future looked incredibly bright.

Connect with the Author

I really hope you enjoyed reading Rain on a Tin Roof. For more action romance info, upcoming release dates, and access to free books join the exclusive Suzanne Cass reader club. As an added bonus, you'll get a copy of my FREE STORY.

Solar Flare

http://www.suzannecass.com/contact/

Or you can stay in touch via my website
www.suzannecass.com

Or

Other Books by this Author
Shadows in the Dust
Book 1 in the Colours of the Earth Series

Shadows in Deep Blue
Book 2 in the Colours of the Earth Series

Shadows of Red Earth
Book 3 in the Colours of the Earth Series

Island Redemption
Who will win at the game of love?

Glass Clouds
Her survival depends on a dangerous stranger.

Chasing Bullets
He'd die for her.

Please Leave a Review.

The greatest gift you could ever give an author is to leave a review. You will be helping other people to discover this book and making a difference to me as an Independently Published Author. If you liked this book and want other people to read it to, please leave a review.

Suzanne Cass has always had a fascination with the tough resilience of people who live in our amazing red-dirt country of Australia. Much of her adolescence was spent working as a jillaroo in the Snowy Mountains, forming her love of enigmatic, outback heroes in wild, passionate, dangerous stories. When not writing about the characters inhabiting her head, Suzanne can be found roaming the Perth beaches with her border collie, or encouraging her two sons from the sidelines as they play their respective sports.

CPSIA information can be obtained
at www.ICGtesting.com
Printed in the USA
BVHW030837120122
626068BV00008B/23